Michèle Roberts is the author of ten highly-acclaimed novels including *Daughters of the House* (1992) which won the WH Smith Literary Award and was shortlisted for the Booker Prize. She has also published short stories and poetry, most recently collected in *All the Selves I Was*. Virago will publish her new novel *The Looking Glass* in May.

Half-English and half-French, Michèle Roberts lives in London and in Mayenne, France.

Also by Michèle Roberts

A Piece of the Night ✗
The Visitation ✗
The Wild Girl ✓
The Book of Mrs Noah ✗
In the Red Kitchen ✗
Daughters of the House ✓ ✓ ✓
During Mother's Absence ✗
Flesh & Blood *poetry.*
Impossible Saints ✗

Non-Fiction

Food, Sex & God

Poetry

The Mirror of the Mother
Psyche and the Hurricane
All the Selves I Was

FAIR
EXCHANGE

Michèle Roberts

A *Virago* Book

Published by Virago Press 2000
First published by Little Brown 1999
Reprinted 2000 (twice)

A CIP catalogue record for this book is available from the British Library

ISBN 1 86049 764 0

Typeset in Caslon by M Rules
Printed and bound in Great Britain by
Clays Ltd, St Ives plc

Virago
A Division of
Little, Brown and Company (UK)
Brettenham House
Lancaster Place
London WC2E 7EN

This novel is dedicated to Mme Yvette Drouard

Ce roman est dédié à Mme Yvette Drouard

Author's Note

This novel owes its inception to Michael Taylor of publishers Calmann-Lévy in Paris, who first told me about William Wordsworth's love affair, at the beginning of the French Revolution, with Annette Vallon, and suggested I write a novel about it. I'm very grateful for the inspiration Michael gave me, but he is not responsible for the way the novel is written. It turned into a historical romance which is *not* about William Wordsworth but about his compatriot and friend William Saygood, a wholly fictional character. Similarly, although Mary Wollstonecraft appears in the novel, I have plundered various aspects of her life for my character Jemima Boote. I have made up events and places as well as people, notably the goings-on in the fictional village of Saintange-sur-Seine on the outskirts of Paris. I hope readers will forgive me for the liberties I have taken.

Acknowledgements

I'd like to thank Gillon Aitken, my agent, and all at Aitken & Stone; also Lennie Goodings, my editor, and all at Little, Brown/Virago. Thanks too to Julie Pow, who gave me *A Vindication of the Rights of Women* at a crucial moment. Thanks, always, to Jim, and to my friends in Normandy and the Mayenne who have taught me about French country life now and in times past. Any mistakes are of course my responsibility, not theirs.

Many books helped my research. These three were particularly inspiring: *Fragile Lives – Violence, Power and Solidarity in Eighteenth-Century Paris*, by Arlette Farge; *Footsteps- Adventures of a Romantic Biographer*, by Richard Holmes; and *A Passionate Sisterhood – The Sisters, Wives and Daughters of the Lake Poets*, by Kathleen Jones.

Grateful thanks to Danka Masek who turned my messy typescript into beautiful word-processing.

PROLOGUE

Saintange-sur-Seine

1

In her youth Louise Daudry, née Geuze, had committed a wicked and unusual crime. At that time, autumn 1792, she wanted money very badly, so she put aside her knowledge that what she was doing was wrong and would hurt others. She told herself that virtue was a luxury the poor could not afford. She let herself be persuaded that no one would ever find out.

She had borne the mark of her sin all her life, a fact she could not escape, like an extra rib or a third nipple. Her memory of what she had done deformed her, for it led to her complete loneliness. There was not a soul she could tell of her secret. The worst thing about it was that no one could see or suspect it, for it was hidden inside her and did not show. She was too ashamed to tell her husband and children. She had been lying to them all these years, the sort of lying that involves keeping your mouth shut and not speaking out, and she could not stop now. She was too afraid of the contempt they would feel for her if she told them the truth.

She had been well paid for what she did. Gold coins were flicked into her lap and she had counted them and tested them with her teeth. Enough for a decent dowry. She had been able to marry François after all. She had borne three children and only one of them had died. She and François had survived bad harvests, debts, a couple of revolutions, all the turmoil and harshness life chucked at them. But perhaps it was not life but God who was pursuing her now, catching up with her, closing in on her, irate, implacable? Was it God who had sent her this illness as a punishment? She was only thirty-eight and she was not ready to die. Plenty of people did die in their thirties. Annette Villon had died five weeks ago aged only thirty-six. Louise had gone to the funeral, along with everyone else in the village. She had sat stony-faced throughout the requiem mass, hardly attending to the muttered Latin she knew by heart and of which she could not understand a word, too busy with guilty thoughts of the past to pay much heed to her surroundings and the other people pressed against her in the wooden pew. The unheated church was damp and smelled of mould and sweat. The weather that day was chilly and wet. She thought perhaps the illness had first got her in its clutches then, as she waited, stamping her feet on the cold flags of the aisle, to take her turn to bless Annette's coffin with holy water sprinkled in the sign of the cross, and afterwards, as they shuffled behind Caroline and Maître Robert to the grave.

Sometime after Caroline had stolen trinkets and jewellery from her father's house and run away, Louise fell ill. Her head ached, her bones hurt, her teeth chattered. She sat by the fire and shivered and felt she had jumped into old age. She said to her fifteen-year-old son Antoine: after I'm dead, don't delay getting married, when I'm gone you'll need someone to do all my work around here.

To her thirteen-year-old daughter Marie she said: put more wood on the fire. She repeated this every hour. The cold had got inside her and she could not get rid of it. Her daughter humoured her, piling fresh logs in the grate. Neighbours dropped in, when they could spare five minutes, to help Marie. Louise overheard one of them saying: that's right, give her what comfort you can, she won't be here long, she's had her life, poor thing. Louise shouted to herself: no.

Red flames licked and curled around the heaped wood.

They were burning one of the ancient apple trees which had blown over in the orchard in the recent storm. It smelled as fragrant and sweet as the incense the priest lit in the censer on holy days and swung about the altar, veiling it in perfumed mist. The pungent scent of saints' festivities reminded Louise that if she were dying she ought to make her confession. Just in case hell existed. She thought: I don't want heaven and everlasting bliss, though. Too exhausting. I want to lie face down on the earth and kiss it and then be covered by it and be at peace.

The priest had been in the parish for only a year. He hardly knew her. It occurred to her that he was the one person to whom she could confess her crime committed eighteen years ago. He was bound by his vows not to tell anybody else. He might despise her, but at least she could avoid seeing him and feeling humiliated that he knew. She would not have to face his anger or risk losing his love. What a coward she was. But it was too late to tell anyone else now. Even if she only had a few days left to live, she could not face the rejection which would surely come if she blurted everything out.

She said to François: fetch the priest. I want to confess.

She wasn't important enough to be high up on the priest's list. She waited for three days. On the afternoon of the third day he came. The dog yapped outside in the yard, and the priest pushed open the heavy door and entered, fumbling his way through the dark room towards her, grumbling as he blundered into the edge of the table and nearly tripped over the nearby bench. He sank into the chair opposite hers and sighed. The firelight lit up his pasty face and thin fair hair. He smelled of old sweat. She supposed he had just the one soutane and so it never got washed. He was holding his handkerchief over his mouth, which made her realise she must smell as bad as he. She was too weak to go outside to piss and so she did it into a bucket instead and she knew that often some leaked on to her clothes. She'd stopped noticing the stink in her lap, because doing so made life easier. Now he'd reminded her. But at least he was here.

—Well, Louise, he said: when you're better, perhaps we'll be seeing you more often at Sunday mass.

Louise was silent. She arranged herself into a pose of contrition. She clasped her hands together in her apron and looked down at her feet.

—Well, Louise? the priest repeated: let's get a move on, shall we? I've haven't got all day.

He was undoing his cloak and throwing it behind him on the back of his chair. Underneath he had on the purple brocade stole he wore for hearing confessions. Its two narrow ends, trimmed in gilt, dangled down over his stomach. He settled himself in the chair, squirming his buttocks to get the cushions comfortably dented, then folded his hands one over the other and cocked his head on one side.

—I've got my boys' catechism class after this, he said: so let's give it ten minutes and get it over with, shall we?

They both made the sign of the cross. Louise began with the words she knew so well that they rolled off her tongue like little balls of spit: bless me, Father, for I have sinned.

2

Louise's story reached its climax in France, but it began in England, at Newington Green, just north-east of London. She thought it began there, she explained to the priest, thought you could argue for making it go much further back, like those longwinded genealogies in the Old Testament which traced Jesus all the way from Adam and Eve. So-and-so begat so-and-so who begat on and on for ever. She herself was working the other way round.

To admit to the crime she had committed was difficult. She could not state it baldly. It had to be surrounded with other facts, but then these demanded to be arranged in a row seemingly as logical as those begettings of wise men and prophets. She had to arrange it all in her head as a line of incidents and then speak it. She would have to go back, in any case, to get it right, and to make sure the priest understood. So she decided to recount this part of the story as she had heard Jemima tell it to Annette almost twenty years ago.

—I'm not here to listen to a story, the priest reproved her: I've come to hear your confession.

She crossed herself once more and started again.

PART ONE

Newington Green

1

The eighteenth century's end approached, and with it all kinds of upheavals. In America the spirit of liberty stirred people up to throw off the colonial yoke and demand radical change. In France, the Revolution began to gather momentum. Days of innocence, before the Terror began, when the young believed they could change the world. In England, rioting spelled desperate rebellion against the ancient tyrannies of the landed and the rich. Prophets arose to declare the coming of a new age of justice and enlightenment, or, alternatively, of the end of all things in hellfire and brimstone, lamentations and plagues. Saints who saw the Holy Ghost by night preached their messages in the streets by day. The world glowed like a lamp freshly cleaned, its light divine. Radiance streamed from the heavens and became embodied as angels who were to be seen on Hampstead Heath and Peckham Rye, in Bunhill Fields and on Hackney marshes. You could look up at a tree as you sauntered through Hoxton market and realise that what seemed like a crystallisation of golden fruits was in fact an angel shaking out its wings. Not only poets and holy men saw these cockney cherubim. Jemima Boote did too.

The blustery October morning was crisply blue and gold, the sunlight glittery as glass, smelling of chrysanthemums and

horse dung and hops. Jemima, who had walked down to
Hoxton on an errand for the school cook, heard the rattle of
walnuts hitting the cobblestones. She looked up and saw an
angel swinging her legs in a tree, pelting the stallholders' shoulders and backs. She was picking walnuts off the branches that
framed her and aiming them at the people below, and laughing.
When she noticed Jemima gaping at her she winked, then vanished. Not before the girl had committed her costume to
memory: golden helmet, armour and sandals, feathered white
wings with rosy tips. Jemima bent down and filled her pockets
with walnuts. She ran back to school to tell the cook what she
had seen. She was told off for forgetting to buy the fish for the
teachers' dinner, which was the whole point of her errand.
They would have to have pease pudding instead, with roast
onions as a garnish. The cook set Jemima to peeling the onions.
Their sharp tang soon set her weeping as she knifed off their
skins, which was what the cook intended.

Later, when the dinner was all prepared, and cook was busy
lowering the puddings by their cloth top-knots into the pots of
rolling water, Jemima hid in the back pantry and ate her walnuts. Dipped into the crock of salt on the larder shelf, they
tasted fresh, sweet and oily. Under their gold skins they were
white as toddlers' teeth. When she cracked them they revealed
halves tightly coiled as brains, a black membrane holding them
together. She saved the shells for the little girls in the class
below, who made boats with them. A splinter of wood for a
mast, stuck into a blob of sealing-wax at the bottom of the
shell, a triangle of paper for a sail, and you could voyage off
across the waves of the rumpled tablecloth and be a pirate forcing the cook to walk the plank and drown in a sea of hot gravy.

2

The cook was never quite as unpleasant as she might be to Jemima Boote, as the child was an orphan and knew no better. She gave her a smack from time to time, in the heat of the moment, when she misbehaved, or a shake when she dropped a fistful of knives on the floor or got boot blacking all over her face, but she was equally capable of rough kindnesses. If Jemima got the washing-up done in record time she might receive a sultana-studded bun, hot from the oven, or a twist of cheese pastry. On her good days, the cook was fair. On her bad ones, Jemima tried to keep out of her way.

She was a fulltime boarder at the school run by Miss Mary Wollstonecraft and her two sisters at Newington Green. The brochures describing it as an Academy for Young Ladies made it sound very select. Jemima ended up there because it was cheap. Her parents' death from cholera meant that the family of children was swiftly split up. The younger children were packed off to relatives in Ireland. Ned, the oldest boy, was taken in by his widower godfather in Clerkenwell, who was a lawyer and promised to see to Ned's education, and Jemima was dispatched to boarding school. There was little money to pay for this, and so the arrangement was struck whereby Jemima did her lessons at top speed and helped out with household tasks in between. The pupils were graded by age, into great ladies and little ladies, and Jemima, as a sort of pupil-servant, was in a category all of her own. She did not mind her low status because she had Fanny Skynner to love, and this devotion, into which she poured all the ardour of which she was capable, consoled her for the loss of the parents and siblings she had loved before. Their faces blurred. The pain of remembering them became less. To her surprise and shame, she forgot them quite quickly, for she fell in love on the very first day she arrived at school.

She was the newcomer, and to her child's mind everybody else had got there long before her. She hoped she would be able to catch up, and viewed the front door of the school, with its large knocker, with some alarm.

The establishment was housed in a respectable-looking building shaded by tall plane trees. From their dormitory on the second floor the great ladies could look out on to the Green and the sheep that were pastured there. Miss Everina showed Jemima the view, and the bed allotted to her, which she would share with Fanny Skynner, and pointed out to her the drawer of the chest in the middle of the room in which she could keep her clothes. She indicated the dormitory next door, into which she was forbidden to go, where the little ladies slept. Then she bustled her downstairs, to the classroom. Miss Everina was a thin, anxious woman, with dark brown hair frizzed out around her head, and a nose reddened by a cold. She whisked Jemima to a place on the end of a bench, then took up her own position behind a high desk, rapping with her knuckles on its sloping top to quell the noise. There were only ten girls in the room, Jemima discovered when she surreptitiously craned her neck and counted them, but they made enough noise for twenty. They seemed as cheerful and loud as her little brothers and sisters back at home had been, and were just as ignorant. When called upon to recite their geography lessons they giggled and wriggled and hung their mouths open and groaned. Miss Everina scolded them and sent the worst ones to stand, in turn, on the stool in the corner, the dunce's cap pulled down firmly over their foreheads giving them a very odd look.

—Fanny Skynner, called out Miss Everina: name the principal rivers of England.

The girl next to Jemima stood up. Jemima peered at her with interest. So this was Fanny Skynner, with whom she was to sleep. How pretty she was. Long fair curls fell round her rosy cheeks. Her blue eyes danced. She shot a sideways grimace down at Jemima, a little *moue* of amusement and helplessness mixed. Jemima, instantly bewitched, whispered her the names of the rivers, one by one, so discreetly that the impatient teacher did not hear. When she sat down again, Fanny gave her a grateful pinch, and afterwards shared with her, at recreation, a piece of ginger cake from her tuckbox.

Lesson succeeded lesson at high speed. The ladies were like talking books. Everything had to be learned by heart and repeated out loud. Sometimes they chanted together, like many copies of the same book, and sometimes singly. The teachers picked them out at whim. Miss Everina drove them through geography, parsing and history. Miss Evelina, a plumper and worse-tempered version of her sister, whipped them through scripture and arithmetic. From time to time throughout the day a servant poked her head into the room to report on various misdemeanours of the pupils. So-and-so had left her dirty clothes in a heap under her bed. Someone else had left her pelisse in the hall cupboard rather than putting it away upstairs. These culprits were sent off to bed as a chastisement. Miss Wollstonecraft had expressly forbidden the use of corporal punishment because it did not accord with her principles. She believed in making the punishment fit the crime. Untidy girls had their badly folded clothes pinned to their backs. Girls with sloppy deportment who let their heads poke forwards had to walk round the garden twenty times at recreation. Girls with dirty faces were forbidden to wash for an entire day. But no one was ever hit. There was no birch propped in the corner of the room. No strap. No cane.

Miss Wollstonecraft came in to read evening prayers. Her hair was light brown, and not frizzed like her sisters' but scooped back in an untidy bunch. Her face was pleasant and expressive. She wore a fashionable high-waisted dress in dark blue, with a white muslin fichu around her shoulders. She held the prayer book between big, capable hands, and pronounced the psalm in a deep voice. She said goodnight to the girls as they filed out past her, one by one, and she shook Jemima's hand, welcoming her to the school and hoping she would do very well.

Upstairs, Fanny slithered in under the covers next to her, exclaiming at the coldness of the bed. She curled close to Jemima to get warm. Clasped together like spoons, they were soon fast asleep.

Miss Wollstonecraft's academy was an ambitious one. Not only did the pupils learn enough smatterings of the major subjects to turn them into what Miss Everina called useful women; not only did they receive a thorough grounding in the essential skill of plain sewing; they were also exposed to the revolutionary thinking of their chief preceptress. She spoke with open approval of the approaching end of the tyrannical *ancien régime* across the Channel. She made them study French with her, since she yearned to go to France and see the revolution in the making there with her own eyes. She also talked passionately about the need for enlightened female education, and taught them to imagine the rights of women, which were not yet in existence. She urged them to think less of husband-chasing than of living active and independent lives.

—She's a spinster, of course, Fanny explained to Jemima: we all feel sorry for her because she's so eccentric and lonely. She only talks like that because she can't get a man, my mother says.

They were sitting crosslegged, in their nightgowns, on the floor in front of the schoolroom fire, which they had coaxed back into life. They were making dripping toast. The room was in darkness apart from the small red glow of the fire. Their faces were scorched as they leaned forwards, holding the bread, pierced with forks, to the flames, and their backs were freezing. Draughts knifed in from the ill-fitting window sashes and hustled across the bare wooden planks of the floor.

The other girls were all asleep upstairs. The midnight feast was an adventure: something forbidden. Jemima, forgetting all her resolutions to be good, had fallen in with Fanny's idea. To be singled out by her heroine was so flattering she could not possibly have said no. So at Fanny's bidding she crept into the darkened kitchen to forage in the larder for dripping and bread, and she further earned her new friend's approval by demonstrating how she could get a slumbering fire going again.

The cold pork fat on the hot toast tasted earthy and salty. Its richness clotted their tongues. They licked their fingers, contented as cats.

—We'll get punished if we're found out, Jemima said.

—Yes, but we won't be, Fanny said: the Miss Wollstonecrafts are so busy with their books they've forgotten all about us.

Books to the eldest Miss Wollstonecraft meant philosophy and history. When she was reading she didn't remember where she was. The pupils had tested this on more than one occasion by creeping up to her desk and tying together her shoelaces without her noticing. Books to Miss Everina and Miss Evelina, on the other hand, meant doing the accounts. They would sigh and groan, while supervising the needlework class, over columns of figures which always seemed to add up with unhappy results.

—The thing about Miss Wollstonecraft, Fanny pondered: is that although she's so clever she's like a child. She's so passionate.

This was true. Their head teacher could lose her temper in

a flash when teased too far and even burst into furious tears if the girls tormented her enough.

—And then her clothes, Fanny went on: they're far too fine for a schoolmistress. She looks ridiculous, my mother says. Mutton dressed as lamb. She shouldn't want to be thought well-looking, not at her age. She must be thirty if she's a day.

Miss Wollstonecraft was certainly too tall and too broad-shouldered to be called pretty, too quick with her opinionated replies to be called sweet, too fond of the sound of her own voice to be especially pleasing to the parents who occasionally visited the school to see after their daughters' progress. She was learned; she qualified as a bluestocking, and was therefore fit to have charge of the young; but she had few accomplishments and no polite conversation. The people who appreciated her were the local clergymen, high-minded Dissenters who approved of women with noble minds who read serious books and had ink-stained hands. There were several Dissenting families living around the Green. The school attended the services in their austere little chapel, and the clergymen and their clever wives came to tea with the Wollstonecraft sisters in the evenings.

—Oh, she's not so bad, Jemima said: she could be worse.

—Oh Lord, Fanny said: I didn't realise you admired her.

—Don't be silly, Jemima said: of course I don't. She's much too peculiar.

Jemima had fallen in love with Fanny because the other girl was everything that she was not. Fanny was pretty, easygoing, careless. She was a favourite with everybody. Her blue eyes and long blonde curls drew sighs of admiration from all the visitors to the school. She was generous with her things and gave away her sweets and cakes with a free hand. She was not too clever.

The art of femininity in her was like an essence, a perfume she distilled in complete unconsciousness for the benefit of passers-by. Pleasing others seemed to come naturally to her, part of the charm and spontaneity of her character. Jemima, studying these effects, discovered that hard work was, however, involved. Fanny lavished a great deal of thought and care on matters of dress, so that she always contrived to look, despite her relative poverty, not only elegant but stylish. She got up early every morning to arrange her hair in a seemingly careless mass of ringlets and curls. She adjusted her gowns just so, exhibited a neat ankle in a little boot, always wore discreet ornaments to set herself off. She knew exactly how to tie the ribbon of her straw hat in a bow just under her ear. She saved up and bought herself a pair of black lace mittens which were immensely dashing. She was kind to her daydreaming admirer. She taught her a more becoming way to dress her hair and showed her how to wet her finger with spit and smooth down her thick eyebrows. She bullied her to stop frowning so much and to smile more. She gave her several pairs of used and mended gloves. When Jemima was summoned one morning by Miss Wollstonecraft to accompany her on an errand, Fanny even lent her her new pelisse.

The great ladies and the little ladies alike had been given a half holiday while all the chimneys were being swept. They had to stay in bed, to keep out of the way. Miss Everina came into the great ladies' dormitory and read them *Rasselas*. Miss Evelina read Shakespeare to the little ones. Jemima dressed carefully, with Fanny's critical eyes on her, then ran downstairs.

Miss Wollstonecraft was standing in the entrance hall fastening up a leather satchel containing a fat parcel. It was heavy, so once they were on their way they took turns carting it along.

—I've got to take it myself, Miss Wollstonecraft explained: I could have sent it by the carrier, but it might have got lost. I hope you like walking. We've quite a way to go.

They were heading south along the dusty road lined with ditches that ran down into the City. Carriages clattered past at tremendous speed, forcing them to leap out of the way. Dogs ran out, barking, from the inns they passed. Straggles of cottages were grouped around ponds, under great trees. Then, as they got further in, the houses rose and jostled closer together, the streets became more turbulent and noisy, and it was harder to avoid the piles of filth dumped in the gutters. Miss Wollstonecraft marched rather than walked, lost in her own thoughts, while Jemima toiled along at her side. Once or twice she roused herself to point out a landmark, but mostly she was silent. Jemima was too much in awe of her to speak out of turn. She concentrated on hoping she would not get a blister. Already she could feel a warning warmth on her heel.

In St Paul's Churchyard they paused so that Jemima could admire the springing lines of the vast white cathedral that floated above them, indifferent and serene, like an enormous seagull lounging on the air. Miss Wollstonecraft, suddenly recalled to being a schoolmistress, listed types of columns and pilasters, forms of capitals, designs of architraves, but Jemima hardly listened. St Paul's frightened her. She felt as though she were flying up to the white face of the moon and that it would fall on her and crush her. She was relieved when the architecture lesson ended and they turned away and went into Mr Jackson's print shop.

Opening the door, they plunged into the absence of daylight, the smell of dust, ink, leather and tobacco. Bristling at them through the darkness was a tall shape decorated with tufts. These were eyebrows. The thickest and blackest Jemima had ever seen. These, it soon became clear, belonged to Mr Jackson, the publisher. He loomed up and grunted at them.

—G'day, Miss Wollstonecraft. How d'ye do.

He sounded so fierce and glared so ferociously that Jemima hastily looked down, for fear of catching his eye. Such concentrated frowns must mean that he hated everybody and in particular Miss Wollstonecraft and herself. She thought of Fanny, and how her friend would immediately set to flirting with him, to charm him into submission. She wouldn't let a man get away with ignoring her. Jemima gave a nervous giggle, which she tried to turn into a cough when Miss Wollstonecraft glanced at her.

Mr Jackson pulled out two chairs for them and dusted the seats with his handkerchief. His gestures were quick and deft.

His hands were the confident part of him, Jemima realised.
The rest of him was very shy, as though he did not often talk to
people, just lived here in his cavern-like shop and growled at
intruders. It was a new idea, that adults could be shy like children, and hide behind being surly and taciturn, and Jemima
chewed it over while she watched Mr Jackson out of the corner
of her eye. He kept his head turned away from Miss
Wollstonecraft while she opened her satchel and pulled out
the paper-wrapped parcel inside. He glanced around the shop,
or down at his feet, so that he did not have to look at his visitors, and he shot out his few words in a rumble that was hard to
understand. But his hands, lifting out the pile of manuscript
sheets, moved carefully and neatly, and when he took down a
book from the shelf to show Miss Wollstonecraft the typeface,
he handled it without fuss, resting the spine in one palm and
turning over the pages with a long forefinger. He grunted out
his comments and Miss Wollstonecraft talked eagerly back.

The shop door opened and a young man came in. Mr
Jackson went over to attend to him, leaving Miss Wollstonecraft
to show Jemima the books scattered on the counter-top and
explain words like quarto and recto. Both of them turned to
glance at the newcomer. His profile was very elegant and clear-
cut. Like a profile on a coin, or a cameo, Jemima thought. His
face was pale and austere, as though he were a clergyman. He
wore little round glasses fastened with gold wire, and from time
to time he raised a thin finger and pushed them higher up his
nose. He nodded distantly to the two females who could not
resist staring at him, and then retired to the back of the shop
with Mr Jackson. His voice was low but distinct. Jemima caught
the words *pamphlet* and *Jacobins*.

Miss Wollstonecraft, pulling on her gloves and fastening up
her cloak, shot Jemima a meaningful look.

—That's Mr Godwin, she whispered: the philosopher, you
know. One of the greatest writers of our day.

He was the second writer Jemima had met, if she counted
Miss Wollstonecraft as the first. He looked lofty and severe,

like one of the gods in the book on mythology they had been reading in class the day before. She could imagine him half-reclining on a cloud with a wreath of laurel twisted round his brows and a thunderbolt in one hand. He would be dressed in a tunic and sandals. This came perilously close to imagining him without any clothes on at all. White and shivering with a long white cock. Jemima gulped and snorted. She pretended it was the dust and buried her face in her handkerchief.

Outside, their business completed, they stood in front of St Paul's again, marvelling at the enormous dome puffing upwards in white clouds. Miss Wollstonecraft was relaxed and cheerful now that she had delivered her manuscript to be printed. She swung the empty satchel in her hand. She bought them an apple fritter each from the stall on the corner, and a bag of roast chestnuts, and they sat on the church steps to eat them, the gulls wheeling up from the river to flap overhead and scream. Jemima looked about her at the half-moon of higgledy-piggledy building and shops and was seized by the excitement of being in the heart of a great city, an unknown person in the teeming midst of a vast crowd. She felt courageous and inspired.

—If you please, ma'am, what's your book about? she enquired of her teacher.

Miss Wollstonecraft wiped sugar off her mouth on to the back of her hand.

—Oh, I'll tell you, she said: if you really want to know.

She expounded as they tramped back together to Newington Green. Jemima associated feminism, ever after-wards, with a certain amount of pain and stoicism, the burning skin of her blistered heel mixed with her attempt to go on listening even as she limped.

4

Aged eighteen and nineteen respectively, Jemima and Fanny left Newington Green. Miss Wollstonecraft was no longer there to wish them well, for she had departed from the school to seek her fortune in London as a fulltime writer, but Miss Everina and Miss Evelina oversaw their departure from the establishment and waved them goodbye. Fanny went off to Walworth in south-east London and Jemima made her way to Clerkenwell.

—Don't forget, Fanny said as they parted: you're to come and stay with us soon. For as long as you want. And don't worry about the expense of your board. You can always help around the house, if you like, if you're so anxious to earn your keep.

In Clerkenwell, in the house of her brother Ned's god-father, Jemima sat and sewed. Ned was just down from the university and needed a quantity of new shirts. He was about to move into lodgings and study for the law, and had little time to spare for his sister. His thoughts were all of the glories to come: the triumphs, the fat fees, the good dinners. His godfather was a kind man, but he had recently married again and was too taken up with his new wife to bother much with anyone else, while the lady, for her part, made it clear that the sooner Ned and Jemima were gone the better. So the brother and sister parted one morning with no great demonstration of affection, just as soon as Jemima had finished helping Ned pack his trunk and round up all the bits and pieces he had forgotten. What kept her going through these bleak days was the thought of seeing Fanny again, and the plan for their joint future which had begun forming itself in her head while she sat and drove her needle along the lengthy seams of her work. It was a pleasant vision: Fanny and herself running a girls' school, having first gained teaching experience by going out as governesses, and then having saved enough money to rent a little house in which they would live together in great content. Two devoted friends, an example to their pupils of kindness and love, finding in each other all the happiness their hearts could possibly desire.

PART TWO

Walworth

1

The Skynner family had one servant for all the rough work. Her name was Daisy Dollcey. She didn't mind her work too much, because Mrs Skynner didn't follow her around checking on her as she scrubbed and polished, and left it to her to decide what job to do when. Mrs Skynner didn't have much choice, for she was often laid up in bed with a headache or toothache or a bowel complaint. If the house was kept tolerably clean, and the children got out of the door to school in the mornings, she was grateful, and she showed it by understanding that Daisy liked to be left alone to do things in her own way.

When she was in a bad mood Daisy whacked a broom about the kitchen ceiling to bring down the cobwebs that clung, wavering, to the dusty recesses in the corners, then, having dislodged several large and agitated spiders she would sweep these out of the back door, shouting at them to hurry or she would stamp on them. Another job for angry hours was punishing potatoes by peeling off their skins with savage swipes of her knife, then lining them up for the chop and finally drowning them in boiling water. Since the Skynner family drove Daisy into a rage most days, come dinnertime she was usually ready for the potato ritual, and went at it with ferocity.

The calm that generally succeeded potato murder could be

expressed by swishing a wet mop over the greasy flags of the floor. Grim determination fetched in the coals and cleaned out the grates every morning. Disdain collected up the slop-pails, turds bobbing and loosening in yellow water, and emptied them out the front into the kennel which ran down the middle of the street. Happiness was rare, and Daisy kept it for the afternoons when she might be able to sneak her friend Billy in for a visit. On those occasions, waiting for him to tap on the back door, she would clean the few bits of silver the family possessed: the tankard from which Mr Skynner drank his beer, the spoon given to George at his christening, the dish in which Mrs Skynner served sweets when she had any. Not only the sweets but the dish might be invisible. At times of financial crisis it vanished into the pawnshop.

Housework done according to the Daisy system was not as boring as housework repeated every day, the same set of tasks performed over and over. It let her feel she had achieved something. Spotting, for instance, the amount of dead flies and beetles lying, legs up, on the floor below the kitchen windowsill, occurred at irregular intervals. Goodness me, Daisy would think: what a lot of nasty dirty insects. Making her own decision to sweep up the black monsters and wash the window happened probably about once a fortnight. Suddenly she would decide to do it *now*. Letting the dirt pile up meant you really noticed once you got round to removing it. A sort of game, to see how much dirt and mess you could tolerate. Also it let you feel in control of your work. The Skynners were better than most. Working for them in her carefully slapdash way, she did not feel too ground down. She stood up to them, and to the children, and to Mr George and Miss Fanny, and did imitations of them all for Billy in the kitchen in the evenings to make him laugh.

Miss Fanny, for example. Daisy loved acting out her winning ways. She skipped about like a neat slippered mouse. Fanny wore white muslin as often as she could, though it was heavy on the washing, and lace at the neck of her gowns. At night Daisy

curled her hair for her, twisting up the limp blonde locks with
screws of paper. Fanny was very particular about Daisy doing it
right, and Daisy learned to be so too, for if it was not done to
Fanny's satisfaction she would command Daisy to begin all
over again.

Her face was round and smooth. She tried never to frown,
she had explained to Daisy once, because the lines lingered.
Daisy pranced around the kitchen for Billy, not frowning, minc-
ing, trying not to laugh. She exaggerated Fanny's way of
talking. She prattled in a high, light tone, completely even,
with no emphasis on any particular word, just a flow of charming nothings. To Daisy's way of thinking it was a queer way of
going on, bland as porridge without sugar or salt. But Fanny's
brother George's male friends who came visiting liked her that
way. They found her very pretty, with her rosebud mouth and
fair curls and soft eyes. For Daisy she was too much like a
spaniel, but then, Billy swore his taste ran to big girls with
black hair, and Daisy wasn't setting out to marry Fanny, was
she? One of the gentlemen would have to. Sooner or later one
of them would propose. What could happen otherwise?
Marriage was the business of her life and Daisy could not
blame her for getting on with it as best she could.

So Fanny's manners in company were combed and curled as
smoothly as her hair, and her ideas confined to helping whatever gentleman it was talking to her to discover and maintain a
very good opinion of himself. Her expression, in public,
remained soulful and sweet at all times. She had a way of cocking her head on one side and gazing trustfully and wonderingly
at the man addressing her in a kind of touching appeal. Look
how little and fragile I am! that look said. More than once,
when Daisy was setting down the tea things or bringing in the
decanter of wine or more coals for the fire she had to turn her
head away or clamp her jaws together so as not to laugh. There
would be the gentleman swelling up plump and rosy in the
warmth of Miss Fanny's admiration, wagging his head from
side to side or clasping his hands under the skirts of his coat

behind his back and walking up and down the room, quite beside himself with pleasure and compliments, only waiting for Daisy to be gone and the door clapped shut behind her before he'd cough and take Fanny's hand and lead her to the window to admire the view so that he could whisper naughty nothings into her ear which Daisy heard while eavesdropping outside.

Later on Daisy would be rung for to show him out, and on the way downstairs she'd watch him grow pensive and subside a little as he thought of Miss Fanny's pitiful dowry and wondered whether he'd been rash or indiscreet enough to commit himself without being able to withdraw. And so he'd seize his hat and stick, and bolt into the street without so much as a thank-you, a free man, off at a gallop into the fresh air. And Miss Fanny, when Daisy went back in, would be smiling ruefully at her bird in its cage and chirruping to it. That pensive air didn't fool Daisy. Fanny was simply plotting her next move. How to bind the silken threads of her need ever more tightly around Mr So-and-so's neck. Because his vanity would win. He would find he wanted another dose of charm and flattery and back he'd come, wary, to be sure, all the time thinking he was in control of this discreet little flirtation, but drawn like a wasp to a honey pot. Miss Fanny could be so very sweet when she chose. The gentleman thought her a woman of the world (Walworth! Daisy said to Billy: I ask you!) well used to whiling away a dull afternoon in agreeable male company and thinking no more of it. He wouldn't bargain on being so beguiled that he fell in love.

Her friend Miss Boote, being such a foolish and idealistic young lady, in Daisy's opinion, understood nothing of all this. She treated Miss Fanny like a porcelain ornament, all reverence and tenderness, just like the men did. Miss Fanny's dainty appearance concealed the strength of a ship's hawser but it was only when they tried to get away from her that the men discovered this. Miss Boote was still at the adoring stage. Daisy imitated her too, so highminded and sentimental.

—You'll see her for yourself, she told Billy: she's staying

with us for I don't know how long, to be Miss Fanny's companion.

Miss Boote had arrived windswept and ruddy after her walk across London. Her boots were muddy so she took these off straight away, seeing from Daisy's raised eyebrows that she was not to dirty her clean floor. The two of them took the boots into the kitchen and set them near the fire to dry, and Miss Boote stood in front of it, with her back to it, lifting up the hem of her dress to let the warmth get at her legs, quite as though she was in her own home. She saw Daisy watching her and let down her dress in a hurry.

—You mustn't mind me, Daisy, she said: I've got terrible manners, Fanny always used to tell me so.

Next she was peering at what Daisy had got on the table, the vegetables she was chopping up for dinner. Mushrooms and onions and potatoes. Daisy thought this was altogether too rude, so she showed her upstairs, in her stockinged feet, to the parlour.

Miss Boote was in luck. Mrs Skynner was laid up in her bedroom next door with a headache; Mr Skynner had gone out to fetch a newspaper; and the children were all down the end of the garden digging a tunnel. Miss Fanny was all on her own, lying disconsolately on the sofa with a novel in her lap.

—I thought you were never coming, she exclaimed: I've been waiting for you such a long time.

Jemima bent down to kiss her friend's cheek.

—I was kept longer than I wanted, she excused herself: my brother had so many things for me to do that it was midmorning before I could set out.

Daisy pulled out a chair for her, and sauntered towards the door, not too quick, because she always liked to catch the flavour of a conversation as it got going. There was something so annoying about being banished from the room. She showed her independence by leaving as slowly as possible. She spotted some dead roses in a vase and dawdled by the side table near the door, removing them.

Fanny looked Jemima up and down.

—You look so well, she exclaimed: and you've lost some weight! You look *so* much better.

Jemima said nothing. Daisy dropped the dripping roses into her scooped-up apron and went back downstairs, smiling to herself. Miss Fanny needed to be little, because the gentleman she was chasing needed to feel large. You couldn't suspect a sweet mouse with feathery curls of having ruthless designs on you. Whereas Jemima, poor thing, with her tall, robust frame, and her big feet, was all too obviously a young woman with an independent mind and an active brain. Nothing puts a man off quicker than too much brain, Mrs Skynner had said to her daughter many a time in Daisy's hearing: they assume you're aggressive with it. Daisy feared that Jemima was. She didn't know her place. She argued with Mr Skynner over dinner, quite as though they were equals.

Daisy brought in her ragout of mushrooms. She was rather proud of it, because when you can't afford to eat a big piece of meat every day, as the Skynners couldn't, it's comforting to eat something savoury and rich notwithstanding. Daisy had learned from her mother to call mushrooms poor man's mutton, and thought them every bit as delicious. She served them with potatoes fried up with onions and felt she had produced a feast to impress the most demanding guest. At home her mother used to serve fried potatoes with a ragout of hare, but there were no hares scampering through the alleys and back gardens of Walworth, only foxes and pigeons, and of course Daisy had no trap or gun. She was daydreaming away, remembering that hare – more like a thick sauce than a ragout proper – as she handed round the dish. She hoped there would be some left for her.

Fanny poked with her fork at the fragrant heap of black mushrooms, the slices of golden potato, on her plate.

—Is this all there is to eat? she asked: or is there something else coming? I haven't got much appetite today. You know I don't eat much, Daisy. You've given me far too much.

Why sit down to dinner then? Daisy wanted to reply. She took the dish round and served the others, which mercifully shut the children up from their whining and squabbling. They stuck their spoons in and gobbled in silence. Jemima was the same. She tucked in and ate with relish. That's how you should eat, Daisy thought, when something's hot, even if it's unladylike. It spoils it, to let it get cold.

Jemima put her fork down, though, when Mr Skynner started discussing politics. She was all for the setting up of the republic over in France, and the rights of the common people. Mr Skynner began teasing her. Daisy knew he didn't mean half of it. He just loved an argument. It added relish to the meal, in his opinion, and he would utter, with apparent conviction, any absurdities he could think of that would inflame his guest and lead to a good free-for-all.

—Don't let me hear any of that radical claptrap in my house, he roared now: brood of knaves and rascals, the French, stab you in the back as soon as look at you. Give government into the hands of that lot of scoundrels, and you'd be done for.

So he went on, enjoying himself, speaking with his mouth full, spitting out morsels of potato, trying to rouse Jemima up so that he could have a good punch at her and lay her low. Jemima, flushed, compressed her lips. Daisy saw her taking him completely seriously and getting angrier by the minute. Faint noises came from Mrs Skynner, a faded version of Fanny. Daisy supposed she was trying to remind her husband of the courtesy owed to a guest. Mr Skynner was having none of that. Jemima, unable to see that she was being led like a bear with a ring in its nose, leaped in and put up her fists. Between the two of them they went at it ding-dong, while Fanny sat rigid with distaste and Mrs Skynner crumbled her bread roll to bits. She hated raised voices at any time but particularly at meals, when she could not get away.

—And another thing, Jemima blurted out: the French are so much the friends of the people that they are planning to give women equal rights before the law with men!

Mr Skynner was now openly roaring with laughter.

—Oh, the little hellcat, he cried: the little savage, she'll be putting on breeches next, eh Fan? I can see I'll have to look to my authority in the household with this termagant arrived in our midst. I like your friend, Fan. She'll do you good. Stir you up a bit.

Delighted with his triumph, he took a long pull of beer from his tankard. Jemima was scarlet with rage. Daisy felt sorry for her, but she thought she was a fool, too, to expose herself so, first to her host's teasing and then to his cheerful contempt. She decided to intervene and leaned between the Skynners to remove the dirty plates.

Fanny's plate was still full of food. She prodded at her pile of mushrooms caked in yellow grease.

—This is all cold and congealed. I can't possibly eat it. Take it away.

Downstairs in the kitchen, Daisy scraped Fanny's dinner into the bin she filled for next door's pigs. In exchange she got trotters and a nice bit of crackling that she didn't always feel obliged to serve upstairs. She cursed Fanny in silence, and the whole lot of them. She thought she'd be a radical, given half a chance. Then she went back upstairs with the stewed apples and vanilla custard and left them to it. A little later on, when she heard the children stamping out of the door, she went in with a tray and cleared away, and then she sat with Mrs Skynner, who was feeling very poorly again, while Mr Skynner went out.

Daisy had discovered a while ago that if you sat near the connecting door between the back bedroom and the parlour, and put your ear to the crack in the wainscoting, you could hear pretty well everything that went on. So once she had settled her mistress down with a dose of her medicine, which was a heavy opiate that sent her quickly off to sleep, she stealthily moved her stool across to the door and bent her head over the sewing in her lap. She was curious to hear more of the progress of Miss Fanny's latest romance, and she thought it very likely she was telling her dear Miss Boote all about it.

It sounded more like a quarrel, Jemima's voice tearful and reproachful, Fanny's high and calm saying: don't be so silly, I'd hate to come and teach in a school, it's just one of your mad enthusiasms, you'll be over it in a month. There are far better ways of getting on in life, I can assure you.

This was said in her quick, light tone, which seemed to goad Jemima into some hotheaded jealous speech, because quite soon Miss Fanny was saying: don't be such a child, I'm sure I never imagined you had such feelings for me, you know I hate sentimentality, please stop.

Daisy jumped off her stool and went down on her knees and applied her eye to the crack. She could just make out Jemima with her arms round Fanny trying to kiss the back of her neck, which was all that was presented to her, while Fanny, very affronted, spoke over her shoulder in that pattering voice that seemed to have no feeling in it whatsoever. Daisy saw Jemima move away, and then she was out of her line of vision. Mrs Skynner called to her from the bed, so Daisy pretended she had dropped her cotton reel and made a great to-do of searching for it.

2

Jemima stayed with the Skynners for nearly a year while she tried to sort out what she was going to do with her life. She looked after the children and taught the two small ones their lessons while the others went off to school, and in return she received her board and lodging. She kept Fanny and Mrs Skynner company, helped with the household sewing, and avoided Mr Skynner and his eldest son George as much as possible. George was like his father; fond of a good row. Fanny always disappointed him by bursting into tears too quickly when he began prodding her, but Jemima provided better sport. Unable to resist answering back when pushed, she could eventually be provoked almost to physical violence. Knowing this about herself, she kept out of his way. She stitched shirts for him, just as she had done for Ned. She stuck her needle into his white linen skin over and over again. She was lonely, because she had only Fanny to talk to, and Fanny had changed so much that Jemima hardly knew how to treat her. Fanny dictated the terms of their friendship. She needed Jemima to love and admire her, but was nervous if her over-ardent friend tried to get too close. Just as you'd gently kick away an eager puppy with your foot, she kept Jemima at bay with little snubbing jokes. As soon as she felt the sheep erring too far from the fold, on the other hand, she reached out a hand and drew her back, with just the right question, just the right careless caress. Often, in order to be kind to you, she had to hurt you a little first. Wounding you allowed her kindness to come out. It meant you never quite knew where you were with her, and it meant she was always in control. As soon as you forgot what she was like, and relaxed into intimacy with her, she would stab you energetically with some small remark, apparently innocuous but malicious underneath.

Jemima took to walking over to Store Street, to visit Miss Wollstonecraft in her lodgings. Her tiny sitting room was crammed with books. They perched on wooden armchairs and sipped wine out of teacups and discussed politics. Miss Wollstonecraft's large and lively brain seemed to fly about the universe. She had something to say on almost every subject, though she was not at all shy of saying *I don't know* and then trying to remedy her ignorance. Her eyes sparkled as she talked and she waved her hands in the air. Her conversation was so extremely bracing that sometimes it was like having a glass of cold water flung in your face, but Jemima didn't mind. She craved for sympathy, which she didn't get, but at least her old teacher took her seriously. Whatever she said was snatched, tossed up in the air, caught and played with, embroidered upon. Miss Wollstonecraft required that you answer back and keep up with her. She was quite happy to dominate, and Jemima quite happy to leap along after her. At least here they were out of the soft torpor of Walworth Road. Here the windows were kept wide open, figuratively speaking, and the winds of discussion blew freely about.

—So, the job with the Skynners, Miss Wollstonecraft demanded one day: how are you getting on?

Jemima took a long breath. She hesitated.

—Well, she said: I thought I had invented a completely new system. I believed if I loved the children enough, if I really loved them and bothered about how they felt, then they wouldn't suffer and also they'd be good. They wouldn't need to be naughty.

It hadn't worked. She had poured herself out to the little Skynners, in patience, listening, talking, playing, teaching. She became exhausted, and resentful. Her self leaked away into the children's hungry mouths until there was nothing of her left. Finally she understood the absurdity of her behaviour. The children demanded more and more from her, because she was so endlessly giving, and she grew more and more desperate.

She said ruefully to Miss Wollstonecraft: I've discovered there's no such thing as being able to love children perfectly. I can't love all the deprived children in the world. Giving all of myself away to others does not make me feel better; in fact it makes me feel worse.

She took a swig of wine from her teacup. It warmed her throat and stomach. She felt intoxicated, not just by the wine, but by being listened to. She felt brave enough to blurt out her innermost thoughts, to discover them by speaking them. This was a rare occurrence. It made her feel astonishingly happy.

—I don't think I've been really loving the children properly at all, she said: I've been using them. As though they were me and by loving them I could make myself feel better. I don't think children need that kind of love, an endless flow of attention that leaves the governess drained and empty with no idea how to replenish herself. They don't want an angel of goodness who encourages them to believe they can eat her up with their needs and demands. I don't think children really want to turn into greedy little monsters who imagine themselves omnipotent, but that was what I was helping to create.

Miss Wollstonecraft's little cat jumped on to her knee and she began stroking it.

—You were as bad as me when I started being a governess, she said: I too thought I could change children for the better simply by love. In fact I ended up loathing nearly all the girls I taught.

She smiled. An odd smile. Her lips twisted into a grimace.

—I needed too much love myself, she said: my goodness, when I remember the love affairs I had, and how I sought love from men! Of course they couldn't give me all the love I needed. I see that now.

Jemima longed to ask for details of the love affairs, but did not quite dare. She imagined Miss Wollstonecraft in bed with Mr Jackson, or Mr Fuseli, or any of her other men friends who frequently were to be met with on the stairs, and felt both repulsed and impressed.

—In any case, Miss Wollstonecraft went on: I'm much happier writing articles for a living than teaching. And now I've conceived of the most marvellous plan for what I'm going to do next.

She leaned forward and began telling Jemima all about it.

3

Daisy, on the pretext of doing some extra shopping, had been out with Billy. They had strolled from Walworth in the direction of Camberwell, where Daisy bought some cream and eggs from the dairy. They sat for a while on the Green, under the tall lime trees, watching the cows lumbering about, and then walked slowly back. Daisy didn't want to let Billy go.

—Come in later on, she said: I'll leave the kitchen door unlocked, so that you can just slip in any time you like. Once it gets dark no one will notice you. We'll have some supper together. Nobody will find out.

She wanted to be alone with him. Just the two of them, having a nice quiet time, away from other people's eyes. Arranging to meet was difficult, because neither of them had time off. They had to invent errands which allowed them to get away: Billy from his job as a market porter and Daisy from the endless demands of the Skynners. If they were found out they'd be sacked. It was a serious risk, because if you'd been dismissed without a reference you'd never get another job. The sensible thing to do, Daisy thought, would be to get married. Then at least they could see each other openly at night. She decided to mention it to Billy that evening.

On the way back to the house they bumped into Jemima. Billy smiled at Daisy, touched his hat to Jemima, and ran off. The two women walked on together.

Jemima, being officially a guest, had to be shown into the house the front way. Daisy ushered her up the steps, and banged the knocker. The door opened after a few moments, slowly and cautiously, as though the person behind it did not want to be seen. A face peered out. It was Fanny. One hand balanced against the edge of the door. The other clutched the edges of her frilled pink wrapper. Her big blue eyes swerved anxiously past them and back.

—Oh, it's you, she breathed: I wasn't sure, I—

Daisy pushed forward, drawing Jemima after her. They stepped into a well of noise, as though whoever was in the parlour was being murdered. Daisy shut the door on to the street and took Jemima's cloak.

—Sorry if we disturbed you, Jemima said: sorry if I woke you up.

Daisy thought she sounded disappointed at her friend's lacklustre welcome. As usual, she made up for it. She surged forward and kissed Fanny's cheek. Fanny smiled faintly.

—It's nice to see you back so soon, she said: only—

Jemima pointed at the sitting room door.

—But what's all this noise?

—It's George and his friends of course, Fanny whispered: there's no one to see to them, because Mamma has gone out with the children, and Daisy was so long doing the shopping.

The house shook with voices and laughter. There was a pronounced smell of burnt toast. Fanny looked at Daisy reproachfully.

—I went to bed with a terrible headache just after Mamma went out. I didn't know you'd taken yourself off round the shops. And I couldn't sleep. Then, just as I'd dropped off, half an hour ago, George and his friends started playing one of their terrible noisy games.

She sighed, and put a hand to her forehead. She looked

exactly like her mother. Well, someone in the household had to keep the tradition of headaches alive, Daisy supposed.

Jemima looked at Fanny's white face, at the dark circles under her eyes.

—Why on earth didn't you ask them to be quiet! she cried.

Fanny winced at her loud tones.

—Oh, I couldn't do that, she said faintly.

She looked at her friend with reproach.

—You know they never take any notice of me, she sighed: I'm so little, they just loom up and tower over me and I feel so threatened, I don't dare say a word.

She smiled hopelessly, with a hint of complacency.

—You know I can't bear having rows. It's my nerves. I'd rather put up with the noise. I can't bear it when George gets angry. It frightens me.

Jemima strode to the parlour door and flung it open. George and three friends were lounging by the fire, smoking pipes, feet up on the table which they had dragged closer to the bright coals. The tablecloth had been half dragged off and swept into the heap of black dust left where the coals had been carelessly tipped. The top of the table, in between the young gentlemen's boots, was littered with jars of tobacco, clay pipes, tankards of beer and the remains, on a big plate, of some toast crusts and meat pies. The cooking had been going on in the fireplace, where a toasting fork lolled against a crock of melted butter. The four had their voices raised in a chorus, George conducting them with a half-knitted sock he had picked up from the sewing basket by the fire, still with two long needles stuck through it.

The voices were quenched by the opening of the door. You could tell, by their amazed expressions, that they had not expected to be interrupted.

—Oh oh, look out, boys, George cried: it's the Amazon come to shoot us dead with her mighty weapons of scorn and disdain for the nastiness of the entire male sex.

Pain shot through Jemima that he should see her thus. A

virago. A scolding schoolmarm. She felt very tall and very big. Her feet, in their sensible boots, in particular, felt enormous.

She said in the calmest tone she could summon: good evening, Mr George. I'm sorry to disturb your fun, but Miss Fanny has a bad headache and needs some peace and quiet.

—Then why the hell couldn't she say so herself? George shouted: rather than sending in the general in petticoats?

He turned the sock and knitting-needles into a rifle which he aimed at Fanny cowering behind the door: pam! pam! pam! You're a coward, Fan.

Jemima turned her head.

—Don't worry, Fanny. George is a perfect gentleman. He won't misbehave in front of his friends.

She hated herself for bullying and lecturing him. She felt like a clumping elephant. So sturdy and capable. So strong. So rarely ill. She hated Fanny too, for changing from the lively heroine she'd been at school into this feeble creature who was too ladylike to stand up for herself. Pain and anger whizzed about her head like a cloud of midges.

George swung his feet down from the table, scowling.

—Come on, boys. Let's go and find somewhere else to sit, away from whining and mewling women.

They surged out of the room in a clatter of boots. Their laughter boomed in the tiny entrance hall and then they were gone, clattering down the steps into the street.

The house was so quiet, suddenly, it felt as though it had been muffled, a cover dropped over it, as Fanny would drown the singing of her canary in its cage. The young men's laughter was snuffed out like a candle, and in its place was Fanny's sighing, Fanny's high, expressionless little voice complaining of the dirty, smoky room.

Daisy and Jemima set to. Jemima snatched up the scattered cushions which had been flung about, punched them back into shape, shoved them on to the chairs where they belonged. Daisy got down on her knees and swept the grate, brushing up all the cinders that had flown around when the fire was too

vigorously kicked, the stray coals, the burnt slices of toast.
Jemima gathered up the pipes and tobacco which belonged to
Mr Skynner, set them back on the mantelpiece, heaped the
dirty plates, tankards and cooking tools on a tray, whisked off
the tablecloth. In a trice, the room was tidy again. Fanny rested
her hand on the latch.

—I think I'll go back to bed for a bit, she whispered: my
head is still bad.

She achieved a wan smile for Jemima.

—I'll feel better soon. I'll get up and have tea with you later
on.

Jemima had a few moments to herself before the children
and their mother were due to return. She wandered over to
the window and opened it, to let in some fresh air. The world
outside struck at her senses. The sun was going down.
Children shouted as they were fetched in from their games.
The rumble and clatter of horses and carts wove together with
the shrill voices of the women calling above the traffic, the
cries of the man at the corner selling cakes and pies. Jemima
twisted her clenched fists in her skirts, to anchor herself. She
wanted to fly off, to escape from this stuffy room into the spring
evening, with its tender light and its scent of lime blossom, its
invitation to freedom. She wanted to leave and never to come
back.

So where would I go? Jemima asked herself.

The answer was immediate. Oh yes. She knew.

Miss Wollstonecraft was preparing to go to Paris, to see the
Revolution in the making there with her own eyes, and to write
a series of articles about it which Mr Jackson would publish as
pamphlets. Why shouldn't Jemima do the same?

The children tumbled in, tugging their mother behind them,
shouting and scrapping like a pack of little dogs, and Jemima
fell to, sorting out the troublemakers, sending them all off
down to the kitchen for their supper, and helping Mrs Skynner
to bed.

—George has got his friend Mr Saygood coming to tea, Mrs

Skynner said in her faint voice: but really I feel too low to get up again. Will you look after them, Jemima? Fanny will give you a hand.

—Does she know they're coming? Jemima asked in surprise: I'm afraid she won't be able to get up either because she's not very well. I'm sure she doesn't know George is expecting another guest.

Mrs Skynner sank back against her pillows. She gave a sigh of relief. You could see that all she wanted was to fall asleep, to be blotted out and care no more about anything.

—Well, you must just do the best you can. Now leave me in peace. If I wake up and want anything I'll ring.

Jemima closed the shutters and tiptoed out. She looked in on Fanny, who seemed to be in a light doze. She tried to persuade the children to bed, by dint of coaxing them sweetly. This was her old method. It did not work, because it simply made the children want to stay in her company and have one more story, one more song. So Jemima, determined to act on the revelation she had received during her visit to Miss Wollstonecraft, tried firmness. She discovered that you had not to mind being hated. The children spat at her that she was a beast, a pig, and streamed obediently up the stairs. Jemima felt refreshed. She went into the parlour and sat down with a book of poetry which she had bought that afternoon on her way home, and ignored the heap of mending in the sewing basket. She was supposed to mend the children's stockings but instead she plunged into Young's *Night Thoughts*.

She roused herself, her cheeks hot and her tongue tied, when George came home with his friend William Saygood. George burst into the room in his usual way, boisterous and noisy, while his friend followed diffidently behind. Jemima hastily put down her book and snatched up her sewing.

—Now Jemima, George cried: no more of this *Miss* nonsense by the way, for I'm sure you're as good and strict a sister to me as Fanny's ever been. You're to amuse my guest. He's into deep subjects, like you are, so you'll get on with him very well.

Prattle away to him, there's a dear thing, while I rest my weary limbs awhile.

He flung himself on the sofa, clasped his hands over his stomach, twiddled his thumbs, and pretended to doze.

—Don't worry, William Saygood said: he's just getting up his strength for the game of chess he's promised me later on. Poor George. He's worn out from walking all the way up to Hampstead Heath to meet me and bring me back. Now, the poet William Blake would sympathise. He gets a stomach ache every time he goes anywhere near Hampstead. It's the air up there. It's too pure and relaxing.

This was the first time Jemima had entertained a young man to tea. She felt stupid, and shy.

—I've never met a poet, she said, plying her needle: only writers of prose. They seem to be excellent walkers.

William clearly forgave her for this ridiculous speech. He crossed the room and sat down next to her.

She liked his face. Without being handsome, it was pleasing, because it was open and gentle. She soon felt at home with him. He began asking her questions about herself, about school and what she had studied there, and he listened intently to her replies. From the education of women it was but a short step to ideas of radical reform, and from there to a discussion of the Revolution bursting forth in France. William was ardently in favour.

—The old feudal system is rotten to the core, he declared: it must be destroyed and swept away so that the nation can renew itself. One thing's certain. With the King and Queen forced to leave Versailles and move into Paris, the people have shown that their will can triumph. The coming changes are like a force of nature, like a flood or a landslide – they can't be stopped.

—If only they go far enough in the right direction, Jemima said: and let women play a full part.

—You are the guardians of the future, William said: the French place a high value on motherhood. They understand the contribution women make, never fear.

Jemima set down her needle.

—I didn't mean only as mothers. I meant as citizens.

—Oh well, that too, William said politely: I'm sure they're thinking of it.

—*The Rights of Women* by Miss Wollstonecraft, Jemima said: have you read it?

—Not yet, William said: but I'm always meaning to, I assure you. I've met Miss Wollstonecraft once or twice at parties. My God, what an amazing woman. These feminists are really fierce.

—I'm a feminist too, Jemima said, sitting upright and speaking rather loudly: I agree with everything Miss Wollstonecraft says.

William laughed.

—No, I meant she's a *real* feminist. She's really terrifying. If you said something she disagreed with she looked at you as though she'd like to chop your head off. Whereas you, Miss Boote, are far too charming to make common cause with those Amazons.

Jemima was silenced. She did not know what to say. Yes, I insist I am one of those frightening unfeminine viragos. No I am not, I am a coward and a traitor, because I care for your good opinion. Oh dear, oh dear.

While she was struggling and speechless, the door opened and Fanny came in. She had washed her face and tidied her hair and dressed herself becomingly in her white Sunday gown, newly ironed by Jemima that morning. Her eyes were sparkling shyly as she looked around.

—Oh, she breathed: George dear, forgive me for interrupting you, I just came to ask Jemima if she would help me with the tea-tray. It's rather too heavy for me to manage all on my own.

George groaned, opened his eyes, and sat up.

—Where's Daisy? he asked: why have you been making the tea?

—Oh, she's downstairs, Fanny said: but I couldn't wait for her to do it all by herself. We wouldn't have had tea before mid-

night at that rate. She's still polishing the silver and I don't
know what else. She's in a great sulk and fluster because she's
so behind. Poor thing, I didn't want to add to her labours, so I
made the tea myself.

Her smile was for William, though her words were addressed
to George.

—You'll have to ask your friend to forgive us for bothering
him with our domestic affairs. But I'm sure you warned him
how very simply we live.

—George, said William, springing to his feet: won't you
introduce me to your sister?

George snorted. He was clearly unimpressed by Fanny's display of solicitude for the overworked Daisy. Now he was
punishing her for her artful and graceful ways. He performed
the introduction as briefly as possible.

—Fanny, this is Mr William Saygood.

William pretended not to notice George's brusqueness.
Jemima watched him make a little bow to Fanny and smile
down at her, while she blushed and bobbed. How appealing
she looked, with her blonde curls piled up and fastened with a
knot of ribbon, her drooping lips lifting into a tremulous smile,
and her dimples showing. William gazed at her as though she
were a rare plant, a precious flower.

—My sister Polly's just like you, he said: she's always trying
to help people with their burdens.

Fanny pouted.

—Oh, I'm hopeless. I can't even carry a tea-tray upstairs.

She was standing near the hearth. The flames of the candles
on the mantelpiece cast a golden glow around her head. She
was so little and slender, so fragile, so pretty, that she
reminded Jemima of a fairy in a children's book, one of those
fairies out of Shakespeare, all gauze wings and crowns of but-
tercups. Jemima could see from William's rapt face that he
was enchanted.

She got up, ready to go downstairs and help. But William was
before her.

—Please, he said: let me come and carry the tea-tray for you. I'd be only too delighted.

—Oh thank you so much, Fanny said.

George burst out laughing.

—I see your headache's better then, he cried: that's something, eh?

Fanny shook her head at him in playful reproach.

—Brothers, she murmured: how you do love to tease.

William was back in two minutes. He carried the round table over to the fire, and set the tea-tray on it. He helped Fanny hand round the cups, and the buttered toast. He laughed and joked. He told them about his sister Polly, whom he saw only rarely, in the holidays, whenever they could afford to travel to meet each other. Men were lucky who had sisters. George yelped with laughter at this, but he did not contradict his friend. He sat back and yawned sardonically as Fanny served them all, using her prettiest gestures, her most delicate turnings of head and wrist. Jemima sat still. She sipped her tea and nibbled her toast, and watched Fanny bloom under the sun of masculine attention. It brought out something deeper, calmer, than her recent querulousness. That was it, Jemima thought, watching. She needed William's sex to weigh on hers, like scales in a balance. Like two lovers on a swing, rocking each other up and down, up and down. She was surprised to discover that she supposed William and Fanny to be falling so soon in love, on a mere half-hour's acquaintance. Not that either showed any sign of it. Fanny's manners were far too correct, and in any case, Jemima knew perfectly well, she would be shy of frightening a possible suitor away with too open a show of interest. William, with all the reserve and delicacy of the good manners he had been taught, was nonetheless clearly very impressed with his friend's pretty sister. Fanny was the most demure of sunflowers, tilting towards and revolving around the source of light.

Now she was stirring her tea and looking up at William with her big eyes.

—And so what career do you plan to follow, Mr Saygood? she asked: once you have completed all your numerous degrees?

—My family wish me to take orders, William replied: but I'm going to be a poet. I haven't told them yet. They'll find it rather a nasty shock. The problem, of course, is that poetry does not pay well.

—Nor, necessarily, said George: does being a clergyman. Why on earth don't you go into the army, or study law?

Fanny clasped her hands together and turned to look directly at William, who sat next to her. Her eyes were burning with sincerity.

—To be a poet is to follow the highest vocation there is, she declared: you must let nothing and no one stand in your way.

—Those are kind and noble words, William said, smiling: thank you very much. I shall remember what you say.

—Oh, you like poetry, do you, Fan? George asked: that's news to me.

She smiled sweetly at him.

—That's because you don't discuss with me what I read. You're not interested. You assume girls' books are rubbish. But Jemima and I read poetry together whenever we can, don't we, Jem?

Her eyes dared Jemima to disagree.

—Only today, Jemima said: I brought home *Night Thoughts*, didn't I?

Fanny and William were soon deep in a discussion of modern poetry, or, at least, Fanny managed it so that William did most of the talking while she urged him on with artless questions, hiding her lack of knowledge under a display of ardent interest. William, flushed with delight, began to expound to her his views on how to write. Simplicity, he declared, and clarity, and a contemporary idiom, were the important things. Oh, and an end to pompous Augustan syllable schemes.

—No more fake classicisms, he said: but a return to common speech, the metres of ballads, such as ordinary people use.

—You'll do it, Fanny said: I know you'll do it. A complete renewal of poetry in England. You've got to overthrow all the worn-out, dated models of your forebears. You've got to carry out a revolution!

William seized her hand and kissed it.

—If more readers of poetry were like you, Miss Skynner, the future of literature would be secure. Poets need encouragement to persevere and carry out the deepest longings of their hearts. Your words are like rain falling on my parched earth. Thank you.

Their eyes met for a second. Swiftly, Fanny lowered hers. William jumped up and declared it was late, it was time he was taking his leave.

He shook hands with Jemima.

—Goodbye, Miss Boote. I dare say we'll meet again – on the barricades.

George laughed.

—Paradise on earth, that's what you both think the Revolution will bring. You'll have to banish the serpent first. Or get Miss Wollstonecraft to domesticate him. Put him into petticoats!

William clapped him on the shoulder.

—You're bound to think I'm too idealistic, my dear fellow. All your interests lie in maintaining the status quo. Or so you like to think.

George punched him back.

—Come on. I'll see you out.

William grasped Fanny's hand. He pressed it. He smiled. Then he was gone.

As soon as the men were out of the room, Fanny began to yawn.

—Oh, I'm tired. How he did go on, that young man, didn't he? So full of himself.

This was camouflage. Behind it, Jemima was perfectly aware, Fanny was making up her own mind as to whether or not William would do. She would let them all know, in her own good time, in her own particular way. Jemima was longing to tell someone about her conversation with Miss Wollstonecraft earlier on. She had a new scheme for the future which she wanted to share and to gossip about. But it was impossible to talk more to Fanny that night, mainly because when they descended into the kitchen with the tea-things, Fanny carrying the sugar basin and the tablecloth and Jemima the loaded tray, they found Daisy with her skirts up round her waist sitting astride Billy on a chair. His trousers were round his ankles and his face was full of dazed bliss. Not for long. Fanny's screams roused the two lovers from their grunting trance even as her hands, letting go of cloth and sugar basin, boxed Daisy's ears. Broken china flew everywhere. Sugar crunched underfoot. Jemima, when she tried to intervene, was bundled out of the room by George and told to mind her own business. Afterwards she could not forget the look on Billy's face, of such rapture, such distance from the everyday world, and she could not forget Daisy's straddling legs, so full and white.

The sister and brother acted in brisk concert. George belaboured Billy about the head while Billy dragged up his trousers with one hand and tried to shield his face with the other. Fanny slapped Daisy and shrieked at her. George opened the kitchen door and hoisted Billy out. Then they thrust Daisy down on to a chair and stood over her.

She was not to see Billy any more. She was to have a week's wages stopped, as a punishment, and she was never to clean the silver again, as she could not be trusted. Leaving it spread out on the kitchen table, for that young jackanapes to steal!

But she was not to be dismissed. She would keep her place. Good servants were hard to come by, and Daisy, sluttish as she was, was better than most. It was Billy's fault, for seducing her to commit such a filthy act. So Fanny cried, through her hysterical tears.

Nor would Mr and Mrs Skynner be told of their maid's wickedness or she'd be thrown on to the street. She ought to be grateful that they would go on protecting her, the foul creature.

George pulled at Fanny's sleeve.

—That's enough, for heaven's sake. Come away. Leave the wretch alone.

Where Billy had been, George could follow. Daisy read his face. Easy as a primer spelling ABC. She understood perfectly well why George was agreeable to keeping her on. So when she went to bed, bruised and sniffing, she wedged a chair under the handle of the door. After trying it once or twice, he went away. Then she cried herself to sleep. There was no comfort, with the wound of Billy's loss torn open inside her and all their plans for marriage completely destroyed.

PART THREE

Blois

1

Louise had been dreaming of her lover François. They had been lying together in the dry space on the rocks behind the waterfall watching the white spray fall past, listening to its tumbling splash. What woke her was the rain sprinkling on the sloping glass of the small window set into the roof, light as the scattering of seeds, a hush-hush rattle. With the quilt tucked round her shoulders she floated in a warm cocoon, the narrow bed her ark that glided through the floods. Thinking of François made her melancholy, for he was not here in Blois but back at home, in Saintange-sur-Seine, and she did not know when she would see him again.

The embrace of her warm bed was so seductive that the only way to leave it was violently. She broke free of warmth, throwing back the covers and jumping up to stand barefoot and shivering on the wooden floor. Over the chemise she had slept in she pulled a brown woollen bodice and a blue linen skirt. Country-girl clothes which marked her out, in the street, as a foreigner, but they were all that she had. Underneath she wore linen drawers, a linen petticoat, black woollen stockings. She splashed water on her face, twisted her hair into a knot and crammed her cap over it, thrust her feet into leather slippers, tied on her apron, and then went down, yawning, to the kitchen.

The privy was on the far side of the little yard. She hunched, humming to herself. Back at home, everyone pissed outside, the men behind one barn and the women behind another. You were always outdoors. Here in town the sky shrank to the patch above the washing-line, the street. She missed the green breath of the fields around her parents' house. Here instead of cold fresh earth and plants growing, the air smelled of dust and smoke.

François smelled of himself, a good smell, and lacking his smell brought him vividly into her mind. She had grown up knowing him, in the sense that everyone in the village knew everyone else. He was thin, handsome and impatient. They played together at school. Louise left school when she was twelve and went on learning from her mother at home. Amalie taught her the necessary skills: how to cook, sew, knit, grow vegetables, raise poultry, keep cows. François, like Louise, was also taken out of school, and worked with his father and brothers. They met at those times when everybody in the village laboured together in the fields, but otherwise their lives were separate. Louise's jobs kept her around the farm, whereas François spent much of his time labouring on the corvée, building and renewing roads for the landlord. Everyone detested having to do this. It took up too much time away from their work on the land, it wore them out, and of course it was not paid.

For Louise to be able to meet François away from the watchful eyes of the neighbours, who kept all the young people under strict observation, some planning was required. Flirtations and courtships usually happened at festivals, once or twice a year, so that likely couples got bound into the community's expectations. Louise was going against accepted practice by trying to have a private life. Amalie, had she known, would have warned her: watch out, my girl, you're heading for trouble. But Louise was obstinate and did not care.

She had danced with François for the first time the year before, during the celebrations for Bastille Day. Temporary arches, decorated with flowers, had been erected in the village square. Flower garlands draped all the windows. Everyone feasted together, sitting at long wooden tables in the open air, a banquet provided free by the revolutionary Commune. The dancers, adorned with tricolour sashes, wheeled hand in hand, laughing, around the square and through the streets. Louise was suddenly arm in arm with François, leaping in time with him and the music, feeling the warmth of his eyes on her face. Then he was off, as the circle broke up then revolved and the dancers regrouped in a new pattern, and François was smiling at two other girls, turning to and fro between them.

Louise was full of ardour and hope. The Revolution promised change, that everyone could share in. The lure of liberty was like the dance, snatching you up and whirling you around, your skirts flaring and your tricolour ribbons flying. You spun into newness. You let yourself fall in love and believe in the future. It was 1791. France was poised on the edge of tumultuous adventure and Louise was part of it.

In October of that year she contrived to meet him alone. Once she had decided, all that was required was boldness of action. She simply sent one of the village children to tell him that she would be out early the following morning, picking mushrooms, in the field just below the woods. Then she shrugged to herself. It was up to him whether he came or not, whether or not he minded her making the first move. But, just to be on the safe side, she prayed extra hard to the Holy Virgin before falling asleep: make him come, please make him come.

She went out at dawn, when there was less chance of being spotted by the landlord's agent and accused of stealing. A revolution might be in the making but private property remained private property. Scavenging, however hungry you and your family might be, had still to be discreet. So she crept along the hedgerows, climbing nimbly over gates and ducking under fences, until she arrived in the top field just below the mass of dark beeches on the skyline. The other reason for coming out so early was that it was better to pick the mushrooms before the cows had a chance to stir about too much and trample them, mashing them into the wet grass with their hooves.

She was tired, and hungry for the breakfast she had not had, but she was contented at being out before anyone else. The day felt empty still, just opening up, and so it was full of promise. The pearl-grey sky became streaked with pink. She shivered a little in the cold air but she liked it. The heavy rain in the night meant that her feet were soon soaked. As she stooped over the ground she marvelled at the spiders' webs stretched between the stems of grass, each one gossamer lace jewelled with glittering raindrops. Mushrooms there were in plenty, their round white caps spotting the ground in every direction. She picked them as fast as possible, laying them tenderly in her basket one by one, careful not to squash or damage them.

When, after a while, she straightened up and stretched and looked around at the view, there was François coming up the field behind her.

They did not speak. He helped her, so that she got done in half the time. They did a sweep of half the field each, moving back and forth between the cows and dodging the fresh, wet cowpats.

A light rain began to fall. More of a drizzle than a rain, but enough to wet them through. The basket full, and half an hour won for themselves, they ran into the narrow, tunnel-like lane that separated the hedgerows bounding the pastures. Under the spreading branches of a huge oak tree they could keep dry. François hung the basket of mushrooms from a low branch of hawthorn sticking out of the hedge, and then he and Louise sat down on one of the boulders which tumbled down the bank underneath.

Louise felt so shy she could not speak. François' knee covered in blue cloth was close to hers, almost touching it. She could hear him breathing. The scent of mushrooms enveloped them both. It brought back the recognition of her hunger.

—I'm starving, she said: I wish I had something to eat.

François smiled in triumph. His hand dived into his pocket and came out displaying two slices of bread. He handed her one and she bit into it. Afterwards, when they kissed each other, his mouth tasted of salt and yeast. They walked back down into the village content to be seen together. They had reached an understanding.

Louise, in order to marry, needed a decent dowry. She had two sets of clothes, a feather bed, and a few other bits and pieces, and that was all. François' parents insisted on more, which everyone felt was reasonable. But after so many lean years, Amalie, a widow, had debts, and no money put by. So Louise took matters into her own hands. She joined one of the bands of desperate people who regularly passed by the village, *en route* for the big towns where they hoped to find work and fend off starvation. She avoided Paris and got as far as Blois, where a kindly priest directed her to the house of the Villons, who needed a maid.

Now, inside the house again, Louise riddled the stoves, filled and lit them. Fuel, like everything else in these uncertain times, was very expensive, so the Villons kept just two fires going, one in the kitchen, for cooking and heating water, and the other in the salon, where they ate, sat, and received visitors. The tinkle of Monsieur Villon's bell, once she was back in the kitchen trying to get soot off her hands with soap and cold water, meant that he wanted his breakfast. This early in the morning, he did not take much. A bowl of broth, a piece of bread. She panted into the salon with the tray to find him standing over the stove, reading yesterday's paper. His black brows were clenched over his frowning dark eyes, and his mouth was set in a grim line. He nodded at Louise and made a sound like a grunt. He and his wife were shaken and frightened by the recent events in Paris. They wanted change, but they were moderates, and staunch Royalists. They were content to observe that the privileges of the nobility were being reduced, but that was as far as they wished to go. The news of the invasion of the Tuileries Palace and the subsequent slaughter, the

fact that the King was now in prison in the Temple, filled them
with a horror that came close to panic. They discussed all this
in front of Louise, when she waited on them at meals. Since
they would not have dreamed of talking to a servant about anything they considered important, Louise was able to keep her
opinions to herself. Having seen the desperation of the country
people who were collapsing and dying of starvation, she really
could not be sorry that the Royal Family were in jail. She would
have liked to help share out their goods and redistribute them.
She was a good Christian. Hadn't Jesus said to the rich young
man: sell all your goods and give the money to the poor? Louise
believed that Jesus would have been a revolutionary, were he
alive now. There was no conflict in her conscience between
serving God and supporting the Revolution. She could not
understand the priests who had made such a fuss about taking
the Convention oath of loyalty to the state. The Villons had
been up in arms about it, of course.

Louise kept her head down. She set out Monsieur Villon's
breakfast things on the table, then departed with her tray. A
little later, from the kitchen, she heard his footsteps ring out on
the tiled floor of the hallway. The front door scraped open then
slammed shut. She hoped he would recover his good temper
before he set to work on a patient. She imagined his hand slip-
ping, the scalpel slashing too deep, the gouts of blood welling
from the wound.

She was on her knees scrubbing the kitchen floor when her
employer's wife tapped downstairs and put her head round the
kitchen door. She rocked from one painful knee to the other, to
shift her weight and get a bit of relief, and looked up. Madame
Villon usually took her breakfast in bed in the mornings, on
those days when she did not get up for early mass, and on those
days when she did, she was back in the salon by eight o'clock
and never came into the kitchen before nine, to allow Louise to
get on. After her breakfast, upstairs or downstairs, she would
ring for Louise to clear the empty cup and dish away, and at the
same time discuss with her what they were going to eat for

dinner and supper and what needed to be bought from the vegetable stalls in the main square.

—I'm sorry to disturb you, Louise, Madame Villon said.

Louise sat back on her aching haunches and wrung out the rag with which she swabbed the edges of the floor, where the bristles of the scrubbing brush were too coarse to reach. The water had cooled and made her wrists itch. It was brown, with bits of dirt floating in it. The rag felt slimy.

—You could do with some clean water, Madame Villon remarked.

—Yes, yes, Louise exclaimed: but tell me what it is you want. You can't have breakfast yet, not until I've done the floor.

—Mademoiselle Villon is coming home today, Madame Villon said: I want you to turn out her room and make up the bed, please, Louise. I realise it makes extra work for you. I hope you'll have time to manage everything.

She spoke so politely these days to her servant. Louise enjoyed not having to be too deferential. It was a small recompense for hours of drudgery. It was a sign, Louise hoped, of other, bigger changes that were on the way.

She laboured to her feet. When you'd been crouched over a scrubbing brush for half an hour, your back locked into place and you had to wrench your bones to move and get going again. She wiped her hands on her apron.

—Miss Annette coming home? But I thought she was due to stay in the convent for another year?

The fact that Madame Villon replied at all to this impertinent enquiry made it clear that there was something wrong.

—There are very few convents left, Louise. Surely you know that. And now even the teaching orders are being suppressed. Mademoiselle Villon was forced to leave her convent six months ago. She has been staying with friends in Orléans and working as a private teacher. But now, I'm glad to say, she is finally coming home.

Louise looked at her bucket and shrugged. The floor would have to wait.

—So she's been all on her own in Orléans for six months! she
exclaimed: however did she manage?

—She was with friends, as I said, Madame Villon returned in
a sharp tone: now, Louise, hurry up with my breakfast and the
shopping, and then please be as quick as you can cleaning
upstairs. The diligence gets in at noon and I want dinner
served at two.

The convent was a kind of finishing school, from what
Annette had said on her last visit home. She had described to
Louise the high-ceilinged parlours in which the boarders prac-
tised their dancing and music. It must be better out than in,
Louise thought: poor thing, I hope she had some fun in Orléans
while she could.

Louise did not like nuns. The convent in the village at home
had been staffed by sickly looking women as miserable as sin.
They owned fields all around and exacted their rents as fiercely
as any aristocrats. When the convent had been nationalised
and then sold, and the nuns laicized and sent back to their
families, Louise had rejoiced, like everybody else, believing
that the house and its lands would now somehow revert to the
peasants who worked nearby. That hadn't happened. A local
lawyer had managed to acquire the property, to add to his
already substantial holdings. People seethed, but could do
nothing.

If Annette was out of the nuns' clutches, that could only be
a good thing. In honour of her return, Louise dusted her room
with care, and put a jug of daisies on the clothes chest.

Henri Villon went himself to meet the diligence from
Orléans that stopped in the main square. Louise followed with
the wooden handcart for the luggage. The long, curved wooden
handles were worn by years of hands closing around them,
pulling; smooth against Louise's palms. The cobbles underfoot were slippery after the rain in the night. Her sabots slid
this way and that, wrenching her feet. She trod carefully, wary
of falling over and twisting an ankle.

Henri Villon kissed his daughter, who had the same thick

black eyebrows as he did. On her they were charming, two sensual surprises marking her forehead. Her eyes were brown, fringed with thick black lashes. Her face, and everything about her, was small and neat. She smiled at Louise, then drew her dark green cloak more securely around her. It might be August but the wind was cold. It chafed against them. They plodded off up the street, the father and daughter in front, arm in arm, and Louise behind, carting the trunk and bags.

Louise had cooked a rabbit for dinner, scented with onions and a glass of wine, and a potato *galette* alongside. She had made a salad, and had arranged apricot conserve around a cream cheese. She hoped Annette would appreciate her efforts. She had had to queue for a long time at the baker's, and again at the butcher's. She had had to race through all her work to serve the dinner on time.

Dr Villon often brought home a colleague from the hospital at dinnertime. They would talk shop while chewing their meat, which Madame Villon's withdrawn expression might have told them was not very nice. Surgery was necessary, of course, but it was not really a subject for gentlemen to discuss in public. Louise would hear her remonstrating with her husband in the evenings sometimes: my dear, there is a time and a place. Madame Villon ate her slices of good red meat with a faint smile on her thin face, to convey that her mind was elsewhere, far above this gossip of sawing and gouging and chopping.

Today it was just the three of them. Louise set the pot of stew on the table and whisked off the lid. The rich smell of animal, a little bit rank, gushed out.

Annette turned so pale she was almost green. She threw her napkin over her mouth. She stood up so fast she knocked over her chair. Then, without being able to speak a word of apology, her napkin still clenched to her face, she blundered out of the room. She left the door open in her haste, so that they all heard her throwing up in the hall.

2

The baby coming made Annette shy of going out. She said she stayed inside because she was afraid of falling on the cobbles in the street and then miscarrying. But the truth was that she did not want to show herself in public and receive the curious or scornful looks of others. She wrapped herself in a light shawl, though it was so hot, to conceal her thickened shape. She sat in the salon and stared out of the window at the garden which she had known all her life. The magnolia tree. The beds of pink geraniums. She looked at them intently as though they could speak and give her advice. She was supposed to be sewing for the baby but half the time she daydreamed. She retired inside herself to some invisible world in which she met someone who made her smile, and sigh, and occasionally cry. Louise, running in and out, could see that Annette had not arrived home at all. She was still in Orléans, and thus was not separated from her lover.

Her parents left her alone for the moment. After the initial scenes of outrage and weeping, they were at a loss. And the news from Paris was so disturbing, the tales of looting and massacres that reached them so frightening, that they declared themselves grateful that at least their daughter was safe. They blamed themselves that she had been seduced. She had escaped the ransacking of the convent by a gleeful and angry crowd of local workers. She had done the sensible thing, in taking refuge with friends. But she had assured them so earnestly, in her letters, that she was happy and well in Orléans, that they had not dreamed she might lack protection and had not imagined they should hurry to fetch her home.

Annette did not stir out of the salon, except to go to bed. She cut out and stitched her dreams, making her life fit her own pattern. The dreams flowed over her hands like the white linen of the baby clothes. They spread out and glittered in the August sunlight. She dissolved into the white cloth she was pinning and was lost. That way she did not have to think about what would happen, or where her lover was, or why he did not write to say he was coming to see her soon. Suspended inside her bubble she did not have to notice the passing of time.

She talked to Louise about all this. She tested out versions of the story on her, as though Louise were the model having the dress fitted on her, while Annette twisted her lengths of white silk this way and that, wrapped Louise's shoulders in white lace, experimented with bunches of white taffeta over the hips. She spat out mouthfuls of pins and spoke fluently, her words unreeling like bolts of satin.

—He is an Englishman. He is a poet. He will become a great poet, I know it. I am going to learn English so that I can speak to him in his own tongue. He is not like my father. He is so much more talkative, and not so stern. He is gentle.

She put her hands together in her lap and rocked them. Her head was on one side, her face smiling and relaxed. Louise was crawling around the room on hands and knees, dusting the chairs, of which there were a great many, ranged along the walls as well as around the hearth where Annette sat. She had to pay special attention to the underneaths, for Madame Villon had a habit of suddenly turning the chairs upside down to inspect her servant's handiwork, and more than once she had caught Louise out skimping on removing the pockets of dust that hid in the wooden crevices.

She imagined Annette and the young man together. They

had met at the house of friends, Annette said. A social evening. Louise could see Annette clearly. She was wearing her pink silk jacket over her best dress of thin linen printed with sprigs of red and pink carnations. She had tied a lace scarf around her shoulders and had a knot of pink ribbons in her little straw hat. She was entering the room, playing with her gloves and glancing at the Englishman and cocking her head on one side.

—But what's his name? Louise asked.

—He is called William Saygood, Annette replied.

Louise shrugged. He had to be called something, she supposed. But it was impossible to say. To herself she called him Guillaume. Or the Englishman.

There had been an entire charm, Annette went on, in meeting a foreigner who spoke French with endearing turns of phrase that were all his own, and a pronounced accent, weighting sentences in odd places rather than letting the words dance lightly along. William had noticed Annette listening to his French, that first evening. Her head bent critically on one side, considering. He had crossed the room and spoken to her, so formally you could tell he had learned his version of her language from a book, along with manners and how to address young ladies you had just met in someone else's drawing room in a French provincial town.

—Mademoiselle doubtless considers that I speak execrably, but I beg her to realise that this is only my second visit to France and that I lack practice in her tongue.

—If practice is all you lack, Annette said: then that is easily remedied.

She pointed to the empty seat beside her.

—Why don't you sit down and practise your French on me? I assure you I don't think it at all execrable.

She rolled her rrs as he could not, and he laughed. She twirled her small wineglass by its stem and felt excited by her own courage. She was not at all in the habit of meeting young men, and here was one who was English to boot, and she had invited him to come closer. As he seated himself she looked him over, as though he were some sort of strange beast come padding across the polished floor to growl and swat her with his paws. He caught her eye and gave her such a simple and friendly smile that she began liking him immediately.

That was his great attraction, she told Louise. He treated her like a friend. He asked her many questions about herself and her life and listened carefully to everything she said in reply. No one had ever treated Annette like this, certainly not a man. Her father loved her, but that was a fact of life that did not need expressing; it existed, like the fire blazing in the grate that was let go out at night because you knew it would leap up, renewed, in the morning. Nor did her grown-up brothers and male cousins have time for her. She was a girl, a nice one as far as they could see, and that was that. William brought alive something in Annette that she had not known needed utterance. He made her feel conscious, for the first time, of how silent she had always been; that women were bodies without speech; you folded your hands and listened to the men at table, or around the fire in the salon, and you resigned yourself to being utterly unknown to them, because they were not interested. But with William, Annette was alive and had a tongue and spoke. She invented her own language as she went along. She discovered what she thought and felt by telling him. It was as though her very body had changed. From being simple, well-formed flesh, that she had both to hide and to display for the sake of others, it now glowed and shone, with a light that had come on from inside. Her soul expanded; she presumed it was her soul that twitched and put out its wings and shook them and glowed with joy; but it felt like herself, all of herself, united and undivided for the first time, fully awake, as her lips moved and she struggled to find the words and then let them run freely out. There was such a pleasure in this conversation, a delight that was physical. She felt that the words leaped off her very skin; birds descending and landing on her; or as though she were sprouting flowers, of all odd things; or as though she had grown tiny wings all over, like fur. She felt she

was making something, talking with William, and the delight of
the experience was that it was mutual. Both of them talked and
both of them listened.

—You know what it was, she said to Louise: he made me feel
like a poet. That talking to him, expressing myself, I *was* a
poet. That's when I knew I was in love. And everything else
that happened just grew from there.

Louise crouched near the fireplace, poking her duster tip,
screwed up, through the intricate wooden lace of Monsieur
Villon's favourite armchair. She yawned.

—Sorry. Go on. I am listening. Tell me about where he lives
in England.

Annette spoke raptly, as though she were reading out prayers
from a holy book.

—He lives in the countryside. It's not like around here, more
steep hills and valleys, and the rivers are not so wide. He
doesn't like the city. Not to live in. He went to Paris first,
before coming to Orléans, and it bewildered him. He's gone
back there now, for a little while. When we are married we'll
live in the country, but not too far from town, so that I'll be able
to go to town when I want, and he will have the peace and
quiet he needs for writing.

Louise stood up. She breathed on the looking-glass hanging
over the mantelpiece then rubbed it. She nudged her duster
into its gilded curlicues. She lifted and carefully wiped the
vases of Chinese porcelain then placed them back in exact
alignment. She tried to arrange her words in the same way, so
that they should not disturb the atmosphere. Something might
break unless she took precautions and stopped it. But the
words just blurted themselves out.

—When are you getting married?

Annette sat upright. Her voice was calm. Her words were
distinct.

—As soon as the settlement is organised and all the papers
and things. Papa will see to it. When *he* comes, Papa will discuss
it all.

The salon was finished. Now it was time to go and cook dinner. Louise moved towards the door.

—A good thing you taught him so much French, then, she said: if he's got to speak to your father.

Annette sighed. It was so much easier to speak to William than to Monsieur Villon. When she had offered to give him French lessons he had simply said *yes*.

William understood, without Annette having to explain to him, that she needed to be able to talk to him. Part of his attraction derived from the way he embarked on a voyage with her into conversation. The real conversation, Annette meant. There was the official one, for which he paid, which proceeded according to the rules of grammar and logic, advancing from easy to difficult; and there was the other one, which lay under it. Eventually the two kinds of talking became the same.

She described it to Louise like a play on the stage. She viewed herself as acting the part of the heroine. Lesson one consisted of drawing up their chairs to the round cherrywood table in the landlady's salon and studying one another while they opened the dictionary and ruled lines on sheets of paper. Annette saw a serious young man with carelessly cropped dark hair, regular features, and a face transformed to beauty when he smiled. His hands holding the pencil were long and well kept. His cuffs were frayed and clean. As though in a mirror, she saw William, while he divided his ruled page into two columns, looking back at herself, a small person with abundant dark brown hair falling in glossy curls over her shoulders. Her brows and lashes were black, her almond-shaped eyes liquid and shining brown. Everything about her was miniature and neat: her rosy mouth, her hands holding pen and ink, depositing them tidily in front of her, her ankle, her high-heeled shoe. She frowned at him, very serious. She had decided they had to start at the very beginning. With *le* and *la* and so on.

—You put the masculine nouns on one side and the feminine ones on the other, she instructed him: and then you learn them by heart for next time.

Also she taught him the pronouns. She recited them and he wrote them down. He recorded her below the surface of the words, her white muslin dress with its blue sash, the pout of her lips, the startling brown of her eyes.

In the second lesson they tackled verbs. This time their chairs were placed closer together so that Annette could oversee what William wrote and correct him as he worked. She nibbled the end of her pen. Her tongue was pink as a cat's. He could hear the calm in-and-out of her breathing. Behind her, the tall clock ticked in the corner. The house was hushed. When he cleared his throat it made a tremendous noise and they both jumped.

He closed his eyes and rattled off the verbs. She was testing him. He got through *to be* and *to have* without any mistakes.

—Now we'll start on regular verbs, Annette told him: we begin with *to love*.

She taught him the words to say and he said them. Into the pauses of conjugations he tucked phrases of falling for her and letting her know, like thrusting sprigs of blossom into her buttonhole, sweets into her pocket.

He missed no opportunity, Annette explained later to Louise, to declare his feelings for me. At first shyly, because his French was not very good, but then with growing confidence. I had to encourage him so that he would go on; it is very difficult to court someone in a foreign language, it takes a lot of practice. And he said that he did not have much time. Who knew what would happen, with the Revolution? And he would have to return to England to secure our future, of that he was certain. His family wanted him to take orders, or he might become a private tutor to some lord, he was not sure. We were conscious, both of us, of hastening towards something as yet undeclared, and yet the time slid by, moment by blissful moment, as though we had every hour in the world to ourselves. The lessons he recited became poems. One line of a rule of grammar, and the next a comment about my eyes, which he said were so brown they were nearly black, like the wild

cherries in the garden outside. Our feet rested side by side
under the table, like happy animals. Our first night lay ahead.
It drew closer and closer. Of course I thought we would get
married first. When he came into the room he would kiss my
hand, quite awkwardly, so then he gave that up and kissed my
cheek instead, which was much easier. He told me all about his
life, his home, his beloved sister. I was to share in all this.
Become part of it. He was so sweet to me. Teasing me, telling
me jokes, listening to all I told him about my life, every little
tendril of my words he seized and twisted up like a curl of
vine, rearranged to make it a garland, a crown of leaves.

   They met every day now, because William wished to master
French as quickly as possible. He spoke sometimes of return-
ing to Paris, to see what was happening there, and at these
moments Annette would shake her head and declare his
French was not good enough yet, he must stay with her in
Orléans a little longer.

   He bent towards her in a gesture of sorrow. I am sorry. I
must go. But I will come back as soon as I can.

   One day she was writing out some useful phrases for him,
the sort of thing that travellers preparing for a journey must
know: how to handle officials and get a new passport. Smooth-
talking politenesses to ease transition. William's fist closed over
Annette's. The pen swerved. A tear puddled on to the page and
ink ran sideways. The pen wrote again, in big watery letters. I
LOVE YOU. It hesitated, and then wrote I LOVE YOU TOO.

   Annette was happy now. She had a place with him, in his
affections, and was quite sure of him. And she made a place for
him, weaving round him a delicate web of imagination and
desire; she drew his portrait in words over and over and gave it
to him; he was beautiful clever good and kind and she wanted
him but could not say so. She translated desire into gestures
and looks. Her hand sliding in and out of the fold of her dress;
her eyes cast down; her mouth sighing and smiling both at
once.

   She went willingly with him into his room and watched

while he locked the door. She sat on the chair and he on the bed. He poured her a glass of wine. He leaned forwards and took her hand then kissed her and the kiss tasted of the wine. They had sealed a pact. Her glass rolled away, unheeded, over the wooden floor.

This was not the version of events she could give her father when pressed to explain what had occurred. She protested: I don't know what came over me, of course I never meant such a thing to happen, but I knew he loved me for he told me so constantly, I think I must have lost consciousness for a while, it was like a dream, I could not move, my limbs had lost all their power so I could not run away.

Louise, listening, understood that Annette had not chosen deliberately to lie. Rather, there were truths that girls could not tell to their fathers. So you did your best to create a version that was acceptable. Annette did not mean to betray William and her passion for him, but she had to re-make it in words that would not outrage Monsieur Villon, that was all, because on his good opinion of her depended her future. She could say: I was weak, I have sinned, I should not have let him but I did not know how to stop him, I loved him so I let him because I knew we would marry, I was fuddled by the wine. She could not say: I opened his shirt and laid my face against his skin, I put my hands on either side of his face and opened my mouth on his, I opened myself I opened I opened. Not just out of shame and guilt could she not say these things to her father, but out of modesty and reticence. The time with William had been sacred to them both and no one else should know of it. They had been private with one another and she would keep secret what they had done and said and felt. Except for telling Louise, of course. That was different. She had to tell *someone*. And Louise was sworn to secrecy.

So the story she repeated to her father was one he already knew. Girls got pregnant and their lovers ran away and left them and all that parents could do was try to limit the damage.

Monsieur Villon wanted Annette to consent to lodge a

complaint against William with the police authorities, but she refused. She pointed out that this would be worse than useless; it would be insulting; since he had only gone away in order to sort out the money needed for marrying. She was, she said, quite happy to wait for his return.

—If you won't do as I say I could have you put away in the lunatic asylum, her father thundered: I could have you locked up in prison. I could send you away to be shut up and live on bread and water for a year or two.

Annette stared at the ground in front of his feet. Her eyes scorched the carpet from under her lowered lids.

—Yes, Papa, she agreed: I know you could. But you do not need to do any of those things. William will return as soon as he can. I trust him.

—You're crazy, her father said.

He did not really believe that she was mad. Her senses did not seem to be disordered at all. She had stood calmly in front of him and looked him in the eye. She had spoken quietly, and stayed in command of herself. She did not need shutting up in an asylum, as far as he could see. He did not know what to do with her.

3

Annette had won a breathing space. A few days and no more, perhaps, while her father weighed up his options. Getting rid of her somehow, by kind or cruel means, was what he now realised he had to do. Louise understood this after her time in this household. In the countryside things were different. It was not regarded as quite such a sin and disaster if a girl fell pregnant. The priest would visit to tell her off and berate her with threats of hell, but this was a ritual the family suffered in polite silence to save his face. Then the two sets of parents would get together and arrange the marriage. Everyone knew who the father of the child was, since everyone kept an eye on young people and knew pretty well what they were up to. The prospective husband could be pleased he had a fertile wife. The girl could be relieved she had found a husband after all. It was all quite simple, and well managed by the families. But here in the town, in a doctor's family, a great fuss and scandal blew up. An emergency.

If I were pregnant by François, Louise thought: I'd be able to marry him.

She had a moment's qualm. Would she? No. His family was so much wealthier than hers and she still had scarcely any dowry at all. She sent her wages home to her mother, to pay off the family's debts. The longing to see and touch François flooded through her so that she stood stock still and covered her face with her duster. Then the idea came to her.

She hurried to the salon. Annette was resting upstairs and Monsieur Villon was at the hospital. Madame Villon was staring out of the window as though the petunias blooming in the pots on her windowsill were of such ravishing beauty that she could not tear her eyes away from them. In fact, Louise was perfectly sure, she was trying to blank all her worries out of her mind and was not succeeding. Her hands were teasing the edge of the muslin curtain, picking at it, ripping open the hem.

Louise coughed.

Madame Villon started and glanced round. She looked guilty, like a child caught out inspecting her own poo in the pot. She raised a hand and languidly touched her hair. She dipped into her range of voices and plucked out a frosty one.

—Yes?

Louise explained her plan.

Madame Villon laced her arms across her belly and frowned. She put her right elbow on her left forearm, cupped her chin in her palm, and visibly pondered.

—Your mother will take in Mademoiselle Villon for the requisite period? You are sure?

It took a while to convince her. Then relief flooded over her features. She separated her hands then struck them together.

—Excellent. Then you'd better go upstairs now and help Mademoiselle Villon pack.

Louise wrote to her mother to expect her. She said no more and did not mention Annette.

Annette wrote a long letter to William in Paris, explaining where she was to be found for the next few months, and managed to post it without her parents knowing. As far as they were concerned, William had vanished from their daughter's life and they were relieved. He might still be idling about in the capital, but they did not seriously expect him to present himself and ask for their daughter's hand. He had passed into the category of villain, they washed their hands of him; their one concern now was to hush up the scandal, and that was that.

PART FOUR

Saintange-sur-Seine

1

The journey to Saintange passed without mishap. By day they jolted over potholed roads and by night they slept in inns, sharing a bed to save money. The other passengers complained about the poor food and the hard beds, but the two girls didn't mind. To them it was an adventure. They kept each other's spirits up. Annette was convinced that once she was at Saintange, William would be able to come and see her. She excused him for not wanting to face her parents. They were, after all, formidable. She and he, together, would work it all out. For the moment, for the sake of respectability and to avoid unpleasantness, she had become a widow, a black cloak furled loosely around her and a wedding ring displayed on her left hand.

As they got nearer to their destination, Louise began describing the village and the farm to Annette. She could not stop herself. In her mind's eye she saw the beloved place and she felt obliged to give utterance to the visions that rose there. At the same time, a little anxious lest Annette not perceive the beauties of the place and consider it in some way too poor or too mean, Louise compensated for any deficiencies in her home by not remembering them.

—All round the village there are beautiful woods, she told her

companion: and in the evenings we can go for walks along the
banks of the Seine. The house is on the side of the farmyard,
with two cherry trees nearby. The other trees are apples and
pears, they're in the orchard. My mother keeps cows. She knows
all their names and will teach them to you, if you like. I don't
know if any of the animals have died since I was home last.

When they reached Saintange it was a short walk from the
centre of the village out on to one of the roads that led away to
the north-west. They turned up a track and trudged along.
Dogs yapped and barked. A woman stuck her head out of a
stone-framed doorway. They had arrived.

The local children had obviously raced ahead of them to tell
Amalie that her daughter Louise had arrived in the village
accompanied by a stranger. A small gang of them loitered by
the gate. Amalie came out to greet the two girls, looking dis-
tressed.

—What on earth's happened? Why didn't you explain in
your letter? she asked Louise: have they given you the sack?
What have you done? And who's this? How am I to feed you
both? There's no money for anything.

Annette became urban and haughty. She drew herself up,
clutched her black cloak tightly around her, and stared off into
the distance. Louise stepped closer to her mother. She saw
how thin Amalie had become in the last year, how much more
grey there was in her hair. Her jutting nose and chin were more
pronounced, but her blue-grey eyes were the same as ever, and
Louise trusted to those eyes, which had watched over her
growing up and filled with tears when she left home to go and
find work.

—It will be all right, she whispered: I'll explain everything,
we've brought money with us. Let's go inside.

She did not want the hovering village children to hear what
she had to say. As it was, the details of their arrival would be
broadcast everywhere.

Annette sank down on to the bench by the door. Her face
was white with the strain of walking so far.

—I'll stay here for the moment, she told Louise: I can't move another step.

She managed to sound contemptuous and cross. Amalie was clearly nonplussed.

—Fetch the young lady some water, she told Louise: and there's some bread she can have if she wants. I've got to go and finish seeing to the animals, I'm behindhand enough as it is. I'll speak to you later on.

She strode away. Annette no longer looked scornful. She looked embarrassed, and as though she were about to cry. Louise fetched her a cup of water and a slice of bread.

—Have something to eat and drink, she urged her: and you'll feel better. It will be all right. It's just that my mother's worried about how to look after you properly. I just need to talk to her and everything will be all right.

They had their conference next day. On the night of their arrival, they simply had supper together and went to bed early. Louise's two younger sisters gave up their bed to the girls and tucked themselves up by the fire. They whispered and giggled about the visiting stranger and her thickened shape. Louise lay awake, planning what to say to her mother.

In the morning, Annette sat outside the door in the sunshine, while Louise cleaned the house. Then she ran her mother to earth in the yard.

—Let me help you, she said: what shall I do?

—The vegetables badly need weeding, Amalie said: the *potager*'s smothered in weeds and I haven't had time to clear it. I'll come and help you once I've moved the cows.

Louise fetched a hoe and went into the vegetable garden behind the house.

The hoe had a good long handle, so that you could swing it without stooping and hurting your back. Louise liked hoeing. There was satisfaction to be had from the work of your arms and back muscles, as the sharp curved blade toothed the rich earth, fitting its edge quickly and exactly under the spread of a weed then lifting it out, roots and green crown, and tossing it aside. She paced up and down the plot, the rows of leeks first, then the beetroots, the carrots, the celery. Sweat dripped down her forehead. She wiped it off with her sleeve.

—Eh-oo, eh-oo.

Her mother's voice, calling her from the near meadow. Louise ran out of the *potager*, pulling the gate shut behind her, and followed the lilting cry. She found her mother standing under the first of the nut trees.

—The hazelnuts, Amalie cried: they've all fallen, already. Give me a hand picking them up, will you?

Louise ran back for a basket. Then they worked together, stooping to collect the nuts hidden in the grass. Your finger found them before your eyes did, closing around the frilled coat, the smooth shell. It was a pleasure to have a change of job. The basket filled rapidly as they rattled the nuts in.

—They're very clean, Amalie said: they haven't got trampled into the mud yet. We were just in time.

The hazel trees had deposited some of their load in the field beyond the fence. Half a dozen caramel-coloured bullocks who had been grazing there were lined up, curious to see what was going on.

—Let's pick up those ones too, Amalie decided.

They dropped down on to all fours and crawled under the fence. They ducked their heads and lurched forwards. Louise crouched and pulled the heavy basket through behind her. Their skirts and petticoats were muddy now. In here the earth was more churned up, because of the bullocks, who crowded excitedly around and had to be waved back. They trod about, playful and curious. Amalie and Louise shouted at them from time to time, to make them keep their distance, and scooped up the hazelnuts, prising them from the ruts of mud by the fence.

—Not so clean, these, Amalie complained: the beasts got to them first, trampling on them.

Nonetheless they filled the basket to the brim. They swung it along between them to the edge of the field, squeezed

between the hedge and the gatepost, and got back into the
potager.

—They're much too early, the hazelnuts, Amalie said: it's
lucky I saw them drop, or I'd have lost them. One week more
and they'd have started to rot in the mud.

She parked the basket by the gate and picked up the hoe.
She went quickly up and down the rows of vegetables, dex-
trously working the sharp blade of her implement in and out of
the earth, scuffing it, lifting up the young weeds by the roots
and tossing them aside. Her arms were brown and muscled.
They did the heavy work, grasping the handle of the hoe and
dancing the long thick pole along the rows of beans. Louise followed her, gathering up armfuls of weeds and piling them,
from time to time, on the wheelbarrow.

Amalie was relaxed, humming to herself as she worked. Now
was the time to ask her. Louise coughed, to clear her throat,
then spoke in a loud voice, the words she had been practising
all morning.

—Annette is in great trouble. Her parents are very angry
with her. She's going to have a baby and her fiancé has gone
away. Can she stay with us until the baby is born? Please can
we help her?

Amalie stopped humming. She turned round and looked at
her daughter. She wiped her hand across her brow before she
spoke, then wiped it on her apron.

—It's perfectly obvious she's going to have a baby. But really,
you should have put all this in your letter. How pregnant is she,
anyway?

—Can we? Louise repeated.

—Who'll pay for it? Amalie demanded: her keep'll cost
something.

Louise knew it was going to be all right. She hugged her
armful of weeds then cast them on to the top of the heap on the
barrow. She stooped and picked up some dandelions she'd
dropped.

—Her family will pay for everything, she said: they're so

ashamed of her, they want her to stay away for a while.

Amalie hefted her hoe and walked down the path in front of Louise, who steered the laden wobbling barrow.

—I'll have to think about it some more, she warned: the decision, it's not easy.

Louise knew that her mother had made up her mind.

—Thanks, Maman, she said.

As they reached the house they saw Annette. She was sitting on the bench by the kitchen door, holding a book in her lap.

She got up and watched their approach. She looked very young. She had wrapped herself in her big shawl to try and hide her pregnancy but there was no mistaking it. Louise turned to go and dump her barrowful of weeds on the bonfire. She watched her mother walk up to Annette and say something to her. Her manner was curt, as always, but she was smiling. For reply Annette grasped her by the shoulders and kissed her on both cheeks. Then the two women vanished together inside the house.

Louise was so pleased to be home again with her mother and sisters that she went about singing and whistling all day long. Despite all the privations of their life, it was the one she had chosen. She felt right when she was here. She moved more easily and felt less anxious. People did not look down their noses at her or hold her at arm's length but simply accepted her for who she was. She belonged here. That was that. People from the village who popped in to welcome her home and inspect the visiting widow lady told Louise how plump and well she looked. They assumed it was the effect of having the job in Blois. But she knew it was because she was back. In her place on the planet, that was how it felt. Her little bit of earth, where she could stay.

Amalie's debts were now almost paid off, thanks to the wages that Louise had sent her every month. She could just about survive with the help of her two daughters who worked the land while she saw to the cows and poultry. Having a paying guest to stay for a while was a great stroke of good fortune.

She said to Louise: since the Villons are paying you your wages to look after Madame Annette as well as paying me for her board and lodging, we'll be able to save some of the money towards your dowry.

She repeated this to François' parents, who agreed that it was a start. They consented to the betrothal of the young couple, and promised to fix a date for the wedding once the dowry was assembled. François could now come openly to Amalie's house. He and Louise snatched half-hours together when they could.

Annette discovered, to her surprise, that she liked her new life. She got on well with Amalie, once she had shown she was willing to join in with the family ways and didn't expect to be waited on like a fine lady. She did what she could to be of use. She strung the beans, peeled the potatoes, scraped the carrots.

Amalie's house curved round her and held her, as a mother's arm holds a baby. Inside, it was like a cave scooped out of the hillside, the walls and ceiling blackened by the smoke from the fire which wreathed up to the rafters then vanished. Annette felt now a trodden earth floor beneath her feet; no tiles, no carpets or polished wood. The casement windows were small, half veiled in ivy. Green light pushed in from the outside. When the windows were open you looked out directly on to the yard in front and the *potager* behind, and you smelled the farmyard smells: earth, wetted by rain; dung and manure. To Annette it was the fresh smell of life; not at all unpleasant. When she threw open her little window and leaned out to see what kind of day it was going to be, she experienced a rush of pleasure at the blowing air, the leeks and cabbages in neat tight rows between the stone walls, the chickens pecking about in the dust, the crowing of cocks, the lowing of the cows. How different from Blois, where the house smelled so clean it was cold, all the furniture was spindly and knuckled, and she was bored most of the time, and lonely. Here, you could not be lonely, not physically at least, because you were never alone. The family lived, ate and slept in the one big room. Next door, on the other side of the wall, were the cowsheds and small sheds for poultry. Across the yard were the bakehouse, pigeon loft, the well, and the pit where rubbish was burned.

Amalie gave Annette a little room, which was normally a

store, off the big room. The main store room was the enormous loft which covered the entire first floor, but Amalie had
used the small one as a kind of larder, where she kept her preserves and cheeses. She and Louise carried these out and put
them into one of the sheds. They got an old bed out of another
shed, where it was stacked in pieces, fitted it back together,
and borrowed a mattress and feather bed to put on it. A hook
behind the door held Annette's scanty wardrobe, and anything
that did not hang up was folded and put away in the chest of
drawers they had constructed out of a couple of crates draped
with a spare piece of cheesecloth that Amalie found when she
rummaged in the dairy. Two sacks on the floor served as rugs.
Annette was completely charmed by this severe décor. She
rejoiced in seeing what you could do without: looking-glass,
pictures, chair. She didn't even have a slop-pail. Like everyone
else, she went outside.

She didn't express her pleasure too openly to Amalie and
Louise, because she would have been insulting them. In a way,
she realised, she was playing at houses, playing at peasant life.
Amalie's landlord, who lived in the big manor house on the
village square, was never going to provide her with a decent
floor that did not turn to mud in winter, not even a few flag-
stones around the hearth. Amalie fought a non-stop battle
against dirt, cold and vermin. She did not need a visiting bour-
geoise to compliment her condescendingly on how picturesque
it all was. Yet secretly Annette loved everything about her new
life. The blood and guts of it.

Amalie had borne three children, so Annette felt able to
question her.

—Does having a baby hurt very much? I'm frightened I
won't be able to stand the pain.

—You stand it because you have to, Amalie replied: and
because you know there's an end to it. You get the baby in the
end. You go through it with the baby, for the baby, it's like a
tunnel, and then you come out of the other end, into the sunlight, with the baby, and you forget about the pain.

Amalie encouraged Annette to take regular exercise, to build up her strength. She made her drink milk straight from the cow, warm and frothing, dipping her ladle into the bucket then passing it across. She got her to eat properly.

The days passed and turned into weeks, each one folding gently into the one before, the one after. Annette swelled up more and more, like a pumpkin ripening. She paced up and down in the dark kitchen on rainy days when the wind blew the smoke back down the chimney, when it was too wet and muddy outside to think of going for a walk, hands clasped under her belly, daydreaming, fretting, humming to herself. But William did not write to her and he did not come.

One night François arrived with news.

—The old convent has been let, he told them: some foreigner's taken it. An Englishwoman.

—English!

Amalie whistled.

—A widow they assume, François said: since there's no sign of a husband, not so far anyway. She's come from Paris. Things got rather too hot there and she decided to take herself off. They're not too keen on foreigners in Paris at the moment.

—From Paris, exclaimed Annette.

She sat up, jolted out of the lethargy which overcame her in the evenings.

—However will she manage there all on her own? Louise wondered: the old caretaker's still next door, I know that, but he's getting so decrepit he won't be able to help her much. What will she do for food? The garden must be completely overgrown, it's been abandoned so long.

—She might need someone to supply her with fruit and vegetables, Amalie said.

—She might need a gardener, François said.

—She might know William, Annette said: she must know William. From what he told me the expatriate community in Paris is quite small.

—We'll go and visit her tomorrow, Louise decided: and we'll

take her a basket of things to eat. We'll get in first, before anyone else has the same idea.

Annette and Louise walked down into the village early the next morning, carrying between them a basket of marrows. The former convent that now belonged to the lawyer was at the end of a short lane that ran off the village square opposite the church. The iron gate in the stone wall had been backed with patches of tin, hastily and clumsily nailed up, so that you could not see in. A precaution against thieves in these desperate times. This barrier made the garden beyond the wall, and the house hidden inside it, mysterious and enticing. In that respect, Louise thought, the tin sheets did not discourage intruders at all. Not being able to see through the gates made you all the keener to get in.

Annette stretched out her hand and tugged on the rope fixed to a curl of iron that swung up almost over their heads. They could not hear the bell ring in the house, but they heard the footsteps that came down the path on the other side of the wall, the squeak of the key in the lock that needed oiling, the scrape of gravel as the gate was pulled open from inside.

A tall young woman with brown hair and alert hazel eyes stood in front of them. Her wide mouth was smiling in welcome. Then, when she saw who they were, her smile shrank and became merely polite. Her dress displayed what Annette's ample cloak tried to conceal. She was heavily pregnant. The two mothers-to-be stared at each other.

—My name is Jemima Boote, said the Englishwoman in strongly accented French: won't you come in?

3

For ten minutes, to get their breath back, they rested in the small downstairs room Jemima had chosen to use as her salon. They sat on wooden stools and took stock of each other. The introductions over, everyone felt shy. Then Jemima, as the hostess, took charge. She obviously enjoyed displaying her command of French.

—Let me show you round the house, she suggested: though perhaps, of course, you've been inside before?

—No, Louise said: never. When the nuns lived here, we were forbidden to come further than the gate. And Mademoiselle Annette hasn't been here long. She doesn't live here. She's just a visitor.

She spoke to Jemima as Jemima had spoken to her, with a certain familiarity. It did not come easily to her with a stranger. She braced herself ready for a snub. Then she reminded herself that Jemima had probably been hob-nobbing with revolutionaries in Paris who had given up most polite forms of address. She was a foreigner, anyway. Perhaps she had never even had to learn the formal codes that had been so hard for Louise to master when she moved to Blois to work for the Villons.

Jemima could not resist shooting a quick glance at Annette, at her wedding ring. Annette was blushing furiously. She too had caught that *Mademoiselle* that Louise had let slip. Jemima's own left hand displayed a gold ring. Louise, cursing herself for her mistake, could not help remembering François' comment on Jemima's arrival: there seem to be an awful lot of pregnant widows around these days!

—Oh, so we're in the same boat, then, Jemima remarked gaily to Annette: it's an adventure, isn't it, to come and live somewhere new.

She sounded too cheerful for a widow, Louise thought. She was being effusive, presumably because she wanted them to like her, and felt nervous. Perhaps she was lonely. Sooner rather than later she would tell them of her real circumstances. She was obviously not the sort of person who could keep a secret for long. Clearly she relished openness and frankness. That was her style. Louise could see Annette starting to respond, thawing from her embarrassment.

They followed Jemima around the ground floor of the house. A corridor ran its length, with a cavernous kitchen rather like Amalie's at one end, and an oratory at the other.

—The old caretaker told me the nuns didn't have mass said in the house, Jemima explained: they used this just for saying their prayers and then went to the village church along with everybody else.

Louise shrugged to herself. She knew that already, didn't she. She'd grown up here, after all, and been taught by those very nuns. She didn't need Jemima telling her about their ways.

She did enjoy roaming over the nuns' house, though, and peeping into what had been, in her childhood, its forbidden places. Not that there was much to see. Two rooms opened off the corridor on each side, identical square apartments with tiled floors and small windows. There was no furniture to speak of. A rickety table here, a broken-backed chair there. A chipped vase on a windowsill laced by spiders' webs. Their boots clacked on the floors and echoed in the emptiness. It was not at all melancholy. The light that filtered in from the garden accompanied them from room to room, exposing each interior which they discovered by walking into it and listening to the silence. Jemima had opened all the casements, letting the scents of outdoors drift in: earth and woodsmoke and apples.

The staircase coiled inside a squat tower opposite the oratory. A pointed wooden door led into it. They twisted round rapidly on the shallow steps slotted in like wedges of cheese, opened another door at the top and stepped out into a corridor that was an exact replica of the one below.

—I sleep in here, Jemima said, panting a little after the climb: look.

She pushed open a door into another square room, a little smaller than the ones downstairs. The window looked down on to the garden enclosed by crumbling stone walls. Beyond were the waving green tips of trees, the start of the woods which rolled to the horizon and filled it. A wood pigeon, invisible in one of the apple trees below, cooed throatily and was answered by its mate. Above, the roof creaked, and the floorboards did too when they walked across them.

—It's all lumber rooms up here now, Jemima said: I found enough furniture to make myself comfortable, and eventually I'll take some of it downstairs.

Louise could not restrain herself.

—I'll help you, she burst out: you can't go lugging tables and chairs about, not in your condition.

Jemima seemed pleased. She turned to her and said: thank you.

Annette was examining the little bed whose four posts supported draperies of printed cotton, very clean but washed out, a faded chintz pattern of red flowers and yellow birds. By the bed was a stool, with a jug and glass on it, and under it was a chamberpot. A ladder stood in the centre of the tiled floor and on this Jemima had arranged her clothes, the dresses folded on the steps and a cloak and jacket dangling from the top. Jemima turned to Annette, smiling.

—I've had to improvise, as you can see. We, I, thought the house was let furnished, but it lacks a lot of things. But I don't mind. It's such a romantic place. I love the thought of a community of women having lived here once. And it's such a well-made house. Look at the thickness of these walls. Look at this beautiful floor.

She tapped it with one foot. The small rosy tiles, hexagonal in shape, were arranged in alternating patterns. Some of them were chipped and scratched, but others had a deep buttery shine.

—I prefer this way of living to what I endured in Paris, Jemima went on in her strongly accented French: staying in a house where the servants disliked me and did so little to help. They resented the fact that I was there at all, I suppose. It was all a great muddle. I thought I'd been taken on as a governess, but when I arrived I discovered the family had fled into the countryside, they were so nervous of what was happening in Paris. They left me no address and so I was all alone. Whereas here, I hope, my solitude is only temporary.

Did she mean the baby? Louise was not sure. She was convinced there was a man somewhere in the background. Sooner or later he would pop up.

—But how did you live? Annette was asking: if your job had fallen through how did you get the money to eat?

—Oh, I was very fortunate, Jemima replied: friends helped me. My former teacher was there, writing articles on the political situation for the English press, and I acted as her secretary. And there was another person she introduced me to, Mrs Helen Williams, who was writing a book, her memoir of the Revolution, I did some copying for her too. Bits and pieces of work. I made just enough to survive.

Annette seized the chance to put her question.

—I too have met some of the English expatriates who have been staying in Paris, she said, speaking as distinctly as possible to make sure that Jemima understood: some of them came on to Orléans, where I was living for a while. It is possible that we have some acquaintances in common. Do you know, for example, have you met, Mr William Saygood, the poet?

She could not speak his name without blushing. Jemima glanced at her. She seemed to understand, without further explanation, the information that she was being given.

—Oh certainly I know him, she replied: he is a friend of a good friend of mine. I know him a little. A most talented and interesting man. Though I must admit we argued whenever we met. Our views on politics, in some respects, were not at all the same.

Annette sighed. Jemima looked earnestly at her, and Annette looked back. Louise watched their eyes talk to each other. Surmises darted back and forth between them. Each silently questioned the other.

Jemima reached out and touched Annette's arm.

—Come back down and see the garden. I've started clearing it, it's really pretty. There's a little arbour, where we can sit. It's so warm. Let's go outside.

The mention of the garden reminded Louise of the pretext for their visit. She had left the heavy basket by the front door. As they walked towards it along the corridor she darted ahead. She pulled off the cloth covering the heaped vegetables and pushed the whole thing forward with the toe of her sabot. Jemima bent down to look, and exclaimed.

—Oh thank you. The food shortages were really bad in Paris. There was so little coming in that everything had to be rationed.

—Things have been very bad here too, Louise said: but at least my mother has her little vegetable plot where she can grow what we need. If you would like her to keep you supplied she will be glad to help. If you are planning to stay for a while, that is.

—Oh yes, certainly, Jemima said: I expect to be here for some little time. I'm hoping to write a book.

She led them outside. They had walked through the garden on arrival. Now they revisited and reinspected it. It was arranged as a parterre, with criss-crossing paths separating the overgrown flower-plots. There were some pink roses and red carnations blooming still, and marigolds, run to seed, scattering yellow in thick drifts around the edges of the beds. There was plenty of work for a gardener to do. François would certainly be needed, Louise thought. Jemima's clearing, which she was so proud of, consisted of tying back some of the creepers and pulling up a few weeds which she had left in a heap. Now she swept fallen leaves off the rustic bench under the little pergola in the centre of the garden, where the paths met. Clematis tumbled overhead and spilled down on either side. Annette and Louise sat down while Jemima went inside to fetch some refreshments.

She served them tea, using some of the precious store she had brought with her from England, for, as she explained to them, she was sure the French did not drink it. Annette, thinking of William, and wanting to like it for his sake, took some cautious sips. She frowned at the pungent and aromatic taste, but swallowed it down bravely. Louise quietly tipped hers into the adjacent flowerbed.

—William told me once, Annette remarked: that in England he hardly ever drinks tea. He's so poor he can't afford it. For his supper he just has bread and milk.

Louise shuddered.

—I could make your supper for you, she suggested to Jemima: and your dinner too if you like. I don't suppose you know how to cook, do you? I could come over and cook and clean for you every day and generally look after things. You won't be able to manage with just that old caretaker. He's much too old to be of use.

Annette looked a bit taken aback at the crudeness of Louise's butting in. But Jemima was smiling enthusiastically.

—That would be a great help. But can your parents spare you?

—My mother, Louise said: she's a widow. I'll run home and ask her, while Madame Annette rests here in the shade. It's too hot for her to walk back with me. I'll leave her here until din-nertime, if I may.

Jemima seemed amused at this way of dealing with Annette as though she were a parcel, to be placed here or there, disposed of neatly, fetched when convenient. But Annette was nodding, clearly ready for more conversation, so Louise sped off and left them to it, drinking the horrible tea.

Louise and Amalie discussed the situation and briskly arrived at certain conclusions, a solution which they were sure would suit everybody. Annette would move in to share the house with Jemima, which would mean that they could have each other for support and friendship as the time of their confinements approached and that Amalie could have her store room back. Annette's money for board and lodging would help Jemima pay her rent, and Jemima would pay Louise for whatever cooking and housework she did. Louise would go on living at home, at the other end of the village, so that she could continue to help Amalie, and would come over each morning with bread, milk and vegetables.

That day she returned with a handcart on to which she had loaded a basket of food supplies, a twig broom, and a can of milk. With the help of the old caretaker she lugged down a table and three chairs from one of the lumber rooms, and set these up in the little salon. Then she cooked dinner. Amalie had sent over a cabbage and some dried chestnuts, so she stuffed the cabbage leaves with these, mixed with bread and herbs, put them in a pot, poured a glass of cider over them, and set the whole thing to cook. In between cooking, sweeping the kitchen floor and setting the table, she wandered in and out of the garden, inspecting the overgrown flowerbeds which were a riot of toppling brown weeds, so that she could snatch at fragments of conversation which floated out from the pergola.

—It's not really surprising, Jemima was saying: that I ended up coming out here to Saintange, you know. William himself suggested it. When he heard that my friends were looking for a place for me to stay, once we had decided that I would go out of the city for a while, he said that a friend of his was going to

Saintange, a delightful place, he was sure, not too far out, convenient in every way.

Annette was sighing wistfully.

—I wrote to him to tell him I was coming here to Louise's family, she said: well, at least now I know my letter got through. One cannot be sure, in these terrible times.

Jemima looked sharply at her.

—But surely, she began: you do not regret the beginning of the Revolution, do you? Surely you must think it's going to change everyone's life for the better?

Annette bridled a bit and her lip twisted. Her voice, when she spoke, was determinedly polite.

—Is that what your book is going to be about?

—I suppose so, Jemima said: in a way. My idea was to write sketches of my experiences in Paris, to record some of the events which I witnessed. I know that several of my compatriots are attempting the same thing, but still I hope that certain of the astonishing developments which took place are worthy of being written about more than once.

Annette's indignation made her sit up and lean forwards.

—I suppose you mean the deposition and imprisonment of the King, she exclaimed: certainly the horror of such a crime can never be too much emphasised.

Jemima drew in her breath. Her eyes sparkled with vehemence. She looked ready for a good argument.

Louise did not want the two ladies to start a fight. That would spoil her scheme. She came forward to help clear away the tea-things and clattered them on to the tray. The interruption gave Jemima time to remember that she ought to be polite to a guest and not harangue her about politics. You could see these guilty thoughts chasing across her face. She coughed, and this gave Annette the chance to turn the conversation.

—I expect you miss all the company in Paris, she suggested: it's rather quiet here for you, perhaps.

Jemima chose wilfully to misunderstand her.

—Oh, she said: I did indeed think the countryside would be

quieter than Paris, but it's not. There's always a row going on, bells ringing, cattle lowing, gunshots, dogs barking, women screaming after their poultry . . . I never heard such a racket in Paris, I'm sure.

—But this house itself must be very quiet? Annette asked: don't you mind it? Do you like being here all by yourself?

Jemima was not yet quite ready, Louise could see, to tell them how alone or not she actually was. She smiled and spread her fingers in the air.

—Oh, the house has its own noises. Already I'm getting used to them. At night, you can hear the timbers of the roof settle and creak, as though they're stretching and shrinking, just like a person waking up. And all kinds of creatures seem to live here and race about after dark. Mice and rats mainly, I think. And then there are the owls. They float past my window and hoot. It's a marvellous sound, so long and cool.

—You need a cat, Louise said: I'll give you one of our kittens. My mother will be delighted, she was going to have to drown them all tomorrow.

Jemima looked amused at Louise's management of her affairs. But she accepted the offer with grace.

As they walked back to Amalie's together after dinner Annette said: what are you up to? You're plotting something, aren't you? Come on. Tell me what it is.

Louise twirled her empty basket and banged it rhythmically against the side of her skirt as she walked along.

—She's nice, isn't she? She'll be a friend for you. You need more friends. I was thinking that perhaps you'd like to move in with her.

Annette sounded fiercer than Louise had ever heard her.

—Don't patronise me. I'm managing perfectly well. I'm just waiting for William to come and then I shall be quite all right.

—I'm sorry, Louise said: I didn't mean to patronise you. I respect you. You know that.

Annette did not look as though she believed a word of it. Her body had stiffened with crossness and her face was red.

—Why should I go and stay with that Englishwoman? she asked: just because I'm pregnant? Why should we get on just because we are both expecting babies? We're not brood mares to be shoved into the same stable.

Louise struggled for words but none would come out of her mouth.

—I think she and I are very different, Annette said: in fact, so different that we might not get on. We would argue about politics, for example, and about religion, I'm sure. She's bound to be a Protestant. She'll have peculiar ideas, and she won't stop going on about them. She's that sort. She loves the sound of her own voice.

—I'm sorry, Louise said: I should never have mentioned it. Forget it. I should never have said anything about it.

Annette's voice changed, and became thoughtful.

—And then, on the other hand, she said: she knows William. That's certainly something.

She turned to Louise.

—She might well be reasonable company. At any rate, if she agrees, I'm ready to give it a try.

4

—My parents can't afford to take you for nothing, François said: and you know they need the dowry to be paid soon. They've got debts, like everybody else.

—It's not a question of nothing, Louise insisted.

They were sitting propped against a trunk in a corner of the attic of the ex-convent. Amalie had commandeered the space as a store room for vegetables. Since François had started working for Jemima a couple of days a week, he was able to visit Louise on the quiet. Louise had come upstairs to lay out the trays of onions for the winter. François had brought up the carrots, and the sand to lay them in. Both jobs done, they reckoned they had half an hour to spend with each other before anyone wondered where they were and started shouting for them. They were sitting on one sack to serve as a cushion and had another one wrapped over their knees. Close together, they gained the courage and confidence to discuss the problems which threatened to divide them.

Louise was close to crying. His tone was so brusque. She knew him well enough to know that this meant he was as upset as she. Neither of them could afford to let on about it, that was all. They didn't have time for such luxuries.

She ticked off the items on her fingers.

—I've got my clothes that I've got on, and a spare set. I've managed to get hold of a feather bed and pillow, two blankets, and a quilt, that's plenty of bedding. My mother will give me a couple of her pots and pans that she can spare, and some cups and plates.

—It's the money that's the problem, François said: it's going to take you so long to save it.

Louise thought: all right, it's clear now, I must get hold of some more money. How on earth?

François was pulling at her clothes.

—Come on. We haven't got much time. You know I love you. Come on then, hurry up.

She looked him in the face and put her hands on his shoulders, scrambling around under the sack so that she faced him. Both on their knees looking intently at one another. She felt powerful and important. She didn't really want to force him to wait, but she enjoyed pretending she did. He was always in such a hurry, whereas she couldn't come if they rushed too much. Today it would be all right, because they had spent time together first. They had worked side by side putting away the vegetables into their winter beds, then they had sat shivering and talking under the sack for ten minutes. Just feeling him sitting next to her, talking, after sharing the work, made her feel ready. Whereas François did not seem to need that. He always wanted to jump on her and that was that. Now, she wanted to make love, because they had been close first. Now, she desired him. She put her arms round him and kissed him, then straddled him and got on top of him. She knew she would come quickly this time and she did. He came just after her, groaning into her neck as she lay collapsed on him. Time for one or two quick endearments and then Annette was shouting for Louise from the landing below.

Everyone was always calling her to hurry up. She walked slowly downstairs looking as cool as she could.

Very quickly Louise felt as though the household had been trotting along for months, rather than merely a couple of weeks. Already she had learned many of the quirks of the house. It needed a bit of tweaking and coaxing, now and then, here and there. For example, there was the dresser drawer in the kitchen, which made a habit of sticking. She learned how to pull it out correctly, to lift it and slide it, having soaped it underneath first, because if she tugged it too abruptly the scanty stock of plates and saucers on the shelves would jump and teeter and threaten to leave their places and crash on to the floor. The back door swelled when it rained, and stuck, and you had to force it open, but not violently, or else the hinges would tear out of the rotted wood of the frame. Jemima had fixed up makeshift curtains in three of the rooms, very pleased with her handiness with a hammer and nails. She had draped lengths of cheesecloth over a pole. So when you pulled the curtains, to open or close them, you had to mount on a stool and gather the material into your arms and slide it along very carefully, or the whole thing slid down too far on one side and collapsed on to the floor. And so on.

Annette helped. While Jemima shut herself away in the

mornings to work on her book, Annette would come into the kitchen and peel potatoes or scrape carrots for the soup they ate morning and night. When Louise brought in the clean washing from the line she had stretched between two of the apple trees in the garden, Annette would sort through the armful tossed on to the table, untangle it and fold it.

—If you fold it carefully, she said: I've discovered you don't have to iron it. Not much, at least.

She demonstrated, holding a pillowcase against her, folding and then smoothing it on her belly. The creases disappeared.

—It's called stomach ironing, Annette said, laughing: this baby's good for something, at least.

The linen yielded to her caresses. She beat it and stroked it, picked it up by its corners, which she called ears, flipped it and bent it. She made a neat, towering pile. Then Louise placed this back in the basket and carried it to one side of the fireplace and set it on a chair, so that it could air for a while.

Annette was playing house, pretending to be married to William. Like children setting up in a disused shed and making dinner for dolls. The charm lay in poking about in someone else's things, deciding what you liked and what you didn't. Louise felt the same. There was a particular cloth she became especially fond of, in thick grey linen. She used it for drying the glasses. She graded the other cloths according to their use and beauty. The oldest and most worn were kept for mopping the floor and drying saucepans. The middle range, from torn-up sheets tidily hemmed, wiped the wet plates and dishes. The best cloth, the oblong one of grey linen, stayed quietly at the ready, on the lowest shelf of the dresser. She had never had a house to organise before, and she was enjoying herself. There was no Madame Villon to give her orders and criticise. Annette had no airs and graces; she was properly humble because of her condition of not being married yet expecting; and she was grateful for everything that Louise did to help her. Jemima, also, was glad to be relieved of domestic tasks she did not particularly enjoy, appreciative of a servant who was kind to her

and did not look down her nose and didn't mind being asked
for things. Louise was content.

They ended up eating dinner together in the kitchen every
day, because it was warm there, and because that meant Louise
did not have to traipse along the corridor with trays of dishes.
Also it meant that the dinner stayed hot.

—What are we having today? Annette would ask, though
she knew perfectly well.

—Potato soup garnished with carrots and turnips, Jemima
would answer.

And Louise would join in.

—No, we had that yesterday. Today it's carrot soup garnished with turnips and potatoes.

Before she ate, Annette bowed her head, murmured a
prayer, then crossed herself. Louise did too. Jemima observed
them. She did not utter a grace herself.

—Why thank God for the soup? she asked Louise one day:
you made it. Your mother grew the vegetables, you carried
them here and cleaned them and cooked them, what's God
got to do with it?

Louise was hurt and offended.

—You need to keep on the right side of *le bon Dieu*, was all
she would condescend to reply: you never know when you'll
need his help.

Annette's faith, like that of Louise, was simple and deep.
She had inherited it from her mother, as a most precious gift; a
standard to live by; a promise of vast and enduring love; and
she intended to pass it on to her child.

—You're never lonely when you know God is there, she
tried to explain to Jemima: during the most terrible times of
trial, when human beings abandon you and let you down and
you feel you've been a complete fool to believe in their goodness, that they ever cared for you at all, well, at those moments
you rest in God, you creep inside him as though he's a secret
cave in a rock, and you abandon yourself to him. But of course
you must believe in him to do that.

—I believe in man, Jemima said: not in God.

Jemima had abandoned her pretence of widowhood. The particular man she believed in was called Paul Gilbert. He was a French man of business living in America, who, fired by the political changes in his own country, had hastened back to France when the Revolution gathered momentum there, to observe developments and take part as much as he could. Jemima described him for Annette and Louise. He was tall, lean and quick-moving. He talked with a drawl. He was handsome and funny. He was talented. He could sketch portraits and write poems. He was involved in various business projects, buying and selling. He lived hand-to-mouth, as they all did. His English was not good, which had forced Jemima to improve her French.

—I would never have got to know him in the normal course of things, Jemima said, wiping a piece of bread around her soup plate to mop up every last bit of juice: but all of us foreigners in Paris were thrown together. Friendships formed very fast. Though Paul wasn't really a foreigner, of course. He just seemed like one. People used to tease him about his American accent.

—And your old teacher you told us of, Miss Wollstonecraft, Annette asked: did you see a lot of her too?

—Not as much as I'd have liked to, Jemima said: she was always kind to me, when we met to sort out the work I was doing for her, but she was very busy. She knew a lot of influential people, and was very involved in political discussions with them. She was writing a paper on female education for one of the revolutionary committees, which she'd been specially commissioned to do; she spent a lot of time talking with all the other expatriates who used to gather at White's Hotel. I wasn't really one of them in the way she was. They were all much older than me, for a start.

She grimaced.

—They were all distinguished, more or less. They couldn't really be expected to bother themselves with someone of only twenty. I hung about on the fringes of their group, but I wasn't in the thick of things, like they were.

—You mean they thought they were in the thick of things, Annette said: who were they, anyway? English, Americans. Foreigners come to gawp at the French Revolution as though it were some sort of carnival. *I've* never heard of a single one of them.

—It wasn't like that, Jemima said: they really wanted to help the cause. They wanted to take part. To serve the Revolution. You don't understand what it was like, for us in England, look- ing on across the Channel. It was almost unimaginable that such upheavals could happen. People had dreamed of such radical change, they'd yearned for it and pleaded its cause: now they believed it was beginning. Of course they felt they had to dash off immediately and see for themselves what was hap- pening. Most of them did get involved. They put themselves at risk.

Annette got up and fetched the dish of stewed pears which was their dessert. She dumped it on the table and sat down again. They did not change the plates but simply wiped them clean with bread. It was less work for Louise that way. She was hard pressed as it was, with two households to look after.

—But weren't you terrified in Paris? Annette asked: I can't imagine how frightening it must have been. The situation's so volatile. Peace one day, mass bloodshed the next. To hear the mob baying in the street for more killing. To know that you yourself could be attacked at any moment.

—It wasn't like that, Jemima returned: that violence last month, the slaughtering and massacres, they were planned, organised, I'm sure of it. It wasn't just a spontaneous uprising of what you call the mob. There was a cold-blooded decision to mobilise them, to whip them up. The people leading them knew very well what they were doing – that was the conclusion we came to.

She shrugged, drawing patterns in the crumbs on the table with her forefinger. Then she looked up.

—You know, I have to admit, I've never been happier.

Annette stared at her.

—Independence, peace and quiet for writing, the chance to change my life, new friends coming in: the Revolution made all that possible. Being in Paris was a good experience for me, not a bad one. I felt history was being made, and I was in touch with it.

She laughed.

—I'm sorry if that sounds melodramatic, but it's true.

—But with all the horror happening out on the streets, Annette insisted: how could you bear it?

—I do feel ashamed to admit this, Jemima said: such a time of turmoil and suffering for so many, and yet at the same time it enabled me to live exactly as I liked. To feel free. It is perfectly true. Outside, in the prisons, people were being butchered. I escaped that fate. I sat indoors and started writing my book. Does that make me a ghoul?

Louise rattled together the dirty plates and dishes.

—You're bearing a man's child, she said: you will become a mother. What will you do when the baby comes?

—I shall earn as much money as possible, Jemima said: and pay a nursemaid to look after it. That's hardly unusual, you must admit. The only unusual thing is that I propose to spend my time writing rather than dreaming up new recipes for puddings.

Louise snorted and turned her back.

—Someone's got to think about what to cook for dinner, she retorted: and there's only so many things you can do with a glut of pears. Why don't you give me a hand this afternoon making the preserves?

Annette was agitated now.

—But Mr Gilbert? Surely you and he are going to get married?

—Oh, Jemima said: I don't think so. I don't think I want to get married. Ours is a free union, based on love. That's the joy of it. Marriage would only spoil it.

Louise began washing up as noisily as she could.

—That may be all right in the big city, she said: but here in the country, if you talk like that people will simply think you're a whore. And that's that.

Jemima grimaced. She took herself off to the room she used as her study and banged the door.

6

The days got shorter. The sweetness and warmth of October diminished as the leaves blew down from the trees. Now, at sunset, the bony shapes of trees could be seen against the wild pink sky. All of them were waiting. The news from Paris filled Louise and Jemima with hope, Annette with disquiet. The King was on trial. Jemima had a letter from Miss Wollstonecraft in which she described seeing him driven in a cortège from his prison in the Temple to his trial at the Convention. People watched from behind closed windows, in silence. There was no noise, save for the occasional beat of a drum echoing in the deserted streets. Mary Wollstonecraft wrote that she knew he was going to his death.

Jemima read the letter to the other two. Annette, who had still not heard from William, increasingly saw the Revolution as her enemy, seducing her man away.

—Liberty, fraternity, equality, she said to Jemima: and where has that got you? Where has that got me? That precious freedom you talk of, it's a freedom for men, not for women. Look at us. Pregnant and having to hide because we're not married.

Hiding, Louise thought, was not the word that she would have used. People in the village were laying bets about which of the two would pop first.

It was late morning, and they were sitting in the kitchen

tying bean plants in bunches. Louise and Amalie had harvested the last of the crop, which would be hung from the rafters to dry. Then, in winter, the beans could be podded and cooked. Jemima, who had come in to get warm at the fire, had stayed to help. The letter was in her pocket. It fell to the ground when she pulled out her handkerchief to wipe her inky fingers before sitting down to help with the beans, and she had not been able to resist showing it to her two companions.

—I didn't come here to hide my pregnancy, she objected to Annette: even if you did. Paul persuaded me to come because I'm English, and England is likely to go to war soon with France. He thought I should lie low for a while.

She pulled tight a knot around a neck of beans.

—And in any case, she added: there were plenty of women involved in Paris. I saw them with my own eyes. It was the women who marched to Versailles and demanded bread. Women have been taking part in the street fighting, in the massacres. Women organised their own clubs. Women even speak in the Assembly.

—Yes, but they are simply supporting the men, Annette insisted: most of them, they don't imagine for one moment that their own lives could ever change. Look at Madame Roland. She doesn't want any women at all in her famous salon, she thinks our minds are too trivial. Why should I admire a woman like that? She apes the men, that's all.

—Some of the women revolutionaries care about their own sex, Jemima insisted: Anne Théroigne, Olympe de Gouge, Madame de Genlis.

Annette bent her head over the bunches of beans. She took up her knife to saw at a piece of string. It flashed like a bright little lance. She gave an impatient sigh then shrugged her shoulders. She blew out exasperatedly through her pursed lips.

—Well, we've survived, Jemima said: so far. And you know, Annette, I like being here like this, having this time together.

—What you mean is, Annette said: getting fatter and fatter. I can't see my feet any more.

—I enjoy being able to talk to each other for as long as we want, Jemima said, sighing: once the babies come, that's it, finished. No more conversations. Mothers don't have time for friends.

—They're not supposed to, Annette pointed out: once you're a mother you have to think about your children. That's what being a mother means. You're not meant to be selfish. Friends are for when you're young, or for when the husbands and children aren't there.

—It's not fair, though, Jemima said: men can go on having friends. Becoming a father changes little for them. Whereas for us, our lives are turned upside down. Nothing can ever be the same again.

She stared at her friend.

—Annette, I'm afraid. What will happen to me once this baby is born? I'll vanish. I won't exist any more. I'll be swallowed up in motherhood.

—That's the way things are, Annette said: unless you're rich enough to afford a nurse. Then there's no problem. Otherwise, you just have to get on with it. That's what being a woman means. You make the best of it.

Jemima moved her feet about, flexing them.

—I want things to be different.

—You shouldn't have got pregnant then, Annette said.

7

The small girl made her way down to the bank of the river, where the *lavoir* was. A thin strip of shingle stretched back to a bank of mud. A thatched roof on four columns had been erected here, so that the women of the village could gather to do their washing with some protection from sun and rain. Louise was with them. She was on her knees on the wooden shelf stuffed with straw, which protected her a bit from the hard and mucky ground, and she was beating with a wooden paddle at the sheets she had dumped in the river, which were heavily bloodstained. She pushed the sheets with her strong arms repeatedly into the river water, lifted them, flattened them down again, forcing the water through the cloth, over and over, to soak and rinse away the blood. She would be here all day.

The child stood on the riverbank above the labouring women and hollered. Louise looked up across the row of bent backs and blinked. She groped to her feet, letting the heavy bundle of wet sheets fall, feeling her bones creak after so long stooped in one position. She walked away from her companions and looked up at the child who leaned over from the lane and yelled.

—The Englishwoman's husband. He's come. With another man. François saw them and told me to tell you.

Louise screamed with laughter. She abandoned the washing and called to her friends she would be back to collect it later. Then she ran up the lane as fast as she could. She was desperate to be at the house when the visitors arrived. She was leaning against the gatepost, redfaced and panting, wiping the sweat from her face with her apron, when the two horsemen trotted into sight. They approached her and stopped. Louise dropped a curtsy, then peered up at the two men. She recognised William immediately from Annette's description. The other man was thinner, swarthier. He sat his horse with an air of impatient nonchalance and grace. Louise thought he looked like a pirate. His eyebrows bristled over black eyes, his lip curled, and his expression was a mix of smile and frown.

The old caretaker came out of his shack. He led the horses back down the lane, to find stabling for them. William and Paul yawned and stretched while Louise unlatched the tall gate and let them through into the garden.

—Not a bad place, said Paul, looking critically around: quite a charming little retreat.

He turned to Louise.

—All right. Take us in and announce to your mistresses that we're here. Monsieur Saygood and Monsieur Gilbert. Go ahead and tell them we've arrived.

Louise looked him in the eye. She felt a great delight break open inside her, a big, simple curiosity to see his reaction to her next words.

—If you please, sir, I should also announce to you a certain arrival. And to you, sir, too.

She smiled into their astonished faces.

—Your daughters were born early this morning. Just before dawn.

They were nearly at the front door of the house. Quite distinctly they could hear a baby's wail. It rose and crescendoed and was joined by another. Paul burst out laughing and clapped William on the shoulder.

—This calls for a celebration. Come on, comrade, let's go in and see them.

8

William was almost crying.

—My little daughter, my poem, my pearl.

He and Paul seized each other by the shoulders. They hugged each other and did a sort of dance, laughing and weeping at the same time.

—This calls for a poem, Paul shouted: and a drink.

He flicked a hand at Louise.

—Fetch us a bottle of wine and some paper and ink and bring them in here.

William was blundering about the salon, tripping over the footstool, tugging the edges of the shutters, picking up and dropping books. He ricocheted between dreamy bliss, uncontrollable smiles and sudden gusts of laughter. It was the relief of knowing that Annette had survived and would live, and the baby girl too. He had stayed away, Louise realised, because he was so frightened.

She scurried down the dark corridor, fetched a taper from the kitchen and went into the room where Jemima sat to do her writing. She raided her desk for writing materials then carried them back to the salon. The young men seized them with whoops of pleasure. The release of tension made them unable to be quiet however much they kept shushing each other. But the wine did the trick. They fell into chairs to gulp it and it seemed to sober them rather than make them drunk. But then, when Louise thought about it afterwards, it was such a very strange couple of days that she could not be sure what was normal and what was odd. These two were certainly enthusiastic fathers. They were clamouring to see their offspring.

—Not yet, Louise cautioned them: they're all asleep. Later, when they're awake. In a couple of hours or so.

—There are two hours before us, Gilbert announced: very well, William, are you ready? A ballad each, on the theme of sacred motherhood, or sacred babyhood, or whatever you will, and the writer of the better of the two to be awarded another bottle of wine.

—But how will you know which one's better? Louise asked: who'll judge them?

Gilbert grinned at her.

—You can, if you like. Can you read?

—Of course I can, Louise said: as long as you both write in French. If Monsieur Saygood can speak to me in French then he can write in it too.

She sounded so serious that Paul Gilbert burst out laughing.

—Of course William speaks French. Stick to your pots and pans, my dear, and we'll stick to our Muses. In quatrains, I think, William, don't you?

William gave Louise a sweet smile. Then he turned back to Paul.

—The Muse is Liberty. She'll send us the verse-forms she wants, never fear. She'll dictate a ballad or a sonnet as the whim takes her. In French, naturally, since she, unlike you, my friend, is fluent in more than one tongue.

They fell to writing. The only sound was the scratching of their pens on the paper, the rustle of the fire, the rain beating against the windows. Louise watched for a moment. She had not heard such a queer way of talking before, but she supposed it was because William was a foreigner. That was what filled his French with such quaint flourishes.

—Liberty is a goddess, she told them: she doesn't have time to write poems. She's too busy making a revolution.

Paul Gilbert flapped a hand at her. She shrugged, and left them to it.

François was waiting for her in the kitchen. He drew a dead woodcock out of the inner pocket of his coat and proudly presented it to her.

—Piece of luck, he told her: it just fell into my hands. Somebody must have shot it, I don't know who. It just fell out of the sky. So I picked it up and scarpered.

—Just what we need, said Louise: I've two extra to feed. How nice of you to give it to me and not to your mother. But don't tell her, in case she's hurt.

They sat together at the kitchen table, discussing the news of the two fathers' arrival.

—Not at all well-off, either of them, was François' verdict: did you notice their shabby clothes?

He had to get back to work on the farm. Today was not one of his days for gardening. He embraced Louise and left. She began to prepare dinner. She sat down with the plump bird in her lap and rapidly plucked it. She took out the gizzards, putting them aside for a sauce, and threaded the bird on to the spit. She took the pot of cooking water from the beans they had eaten yesterday, which she had carefully saved, and made soup with it. She added bread, salt and pepper. Just before serving it she would add a spoonful of cream. To go with the woodcock there were a few potatoes. Nothing else. Then for dessert there was *conserve* of pears. Jemima had not, in the end, helped to make it, which had lowered her again in Louise's esteem.

—That'll do, Louise said to the bird, giving the spit a twirl: I consider that a most respectable feast.

Upstairs, all was quiet. Louise peeped into both rooms. Annette and Jemima slept as though stunned by blows. The infants were also fast asleep, tightly tucked up in their makeshift cots, which were the drawers from the chest. Louise was anxious not to risk waking them. Very soon they would wake of their own accord and cry to be fed, and she could do with some peace. She had a bucket of dirty washing to deal with and the guests' dinner to see to.

She laid them a table in the salon. They wouldn't want to eat in the kitchen and they wouldn't want to sit down with her. She loaded her tray with plates and glasses and carried it in.

The two young men were talking, sprawled at their ease by the fire. The empty decanter lolled on its side and screwed-up pieces of paper were scattered around the hearth. The two finished poems dangled from the mantelpiece from underneath a pair of stones presumably fetched in from the garden to use as paperweights.

—I got beaten regularly at school, William was saying in the fluent and correct French that Annette had taught him: for daring to question my teachers. One day I got beaten four times. Once for asking why I had to read so many authors of the past, twice for asking how it had been decided they were great writers, the third time for wanting to know why I couldn't study the English poets rather than Latin and Greek, and the fourth time for having cried and hidden in the housemaid's cupboard after the previous beatings.

—And yet you still became a poet, Paul remarked with his lazy smile: I dare say it must have been your destiny, to battle so much physical correction and still emerge capable of dashing off immortal odes. Perhaps it was the desire for revenge that fuelled you?

—Perhaps, William said: at any rate, rather than beating my tutor, which was impossible, I pummelled the language instead. I punched it into shape to make my own kind of poems.

Louise picked up the decanter and took it away to refill it. When she came back, the conversation had moved on. She kept one ear tuned to it as she shook out the cloth and arranged it. She was collecting titbits of gossip to make into stories for Amalie later on.

William was refilling their glasses with wine. He was flushed and relaxed. He had loosened his cravat and thrown off his coat. He had run his fingers so much through his hair that his short locks were standing on end.

—I believe that the most unpromising child, he said to Gilbert: given sufficient care and love and guidance, is capable of developing into a kind, good-tempered boy. If you brutalise a child, he will become a brutal man. It's as simple as that.

—Yet you didn't, Gilbert pointed out: you've become a warmhearted fellow who weeps over a novel or a poem as easily as any girl. Particularly if it's your own poem, of course.

William flushed.

—I wasn't as rude as all that about your poem, was I? Forgive me. My enthusiasm for discussing literature carries me away. I become over-critical.

Paul half-drained his glass. He kept his voice light and bantering.

—Forget my foolish poem, which doesn't bear thinking about. Continue with your fascinating theory.

—Children are born innocent, William went on: it's up to us not to spoil them or crush them. They're like plants. They need to be brought up with tenderness, to be fed and watered with love and kindness. Then, and only then, will they be able to blossom into full human beings, the like of which we have not yet seen.

—And that's what this Revolution will deliver, you think? Paul enquired: I fear not, my dear William. What you see displayed all round you is nature brutish and cruel, all men's instincts for killing and violence released. While as for the women! They're even worse than the men. I'm afraid that some of the gross and cruel acts we saw last month, those lewd and obscene outrages perpetrated on the bodies of the dead, are beginning to cure me of the idea that a democracy is at all desirable. The people aren't capable of governing themselves. They need very strict control. Without that, the Revolution will surely fail.

William hesitated. His glance crossed that of Louise. She

looked away quickly, not wanting him to know she was listening. She pretended to be completely concerned with setting the forks the right way round. Yet when William spoke, she was sure it was with a full consciousness that she was in the room.

—You're talking as though the women of the people are simply like beasts. Whereas the women of the lower classes here suffer atrociously. They bear the brunt of their families' poverty. They have no rights and no powers and most revolutionary men do not think they should have them. You cannot completely blame them for feeling outraged, and for expressing that rage when given a chance. I see their behaviour in this light. Their acts of violence and killing are to be condemned, certainly, but they are explicable. The people are not the mob of wild animals your language suggests. They are a mass of individuals who make choices and take responsibility.

—Tell that to those fishwives who helped disembowel the corpses in the Tuileries like so many herrings, Paul responded, laughing.

He watched Louise walk out of the room. She could feel his eyes swivel over her. When she came back in with the tray of food he stared at her again.

—As for educating women, my dear friend, he was saying to William in his drawling French: don't talk to me of it. Who wants to go to bed with a clever woman? I certainly don't. I like them young, fresh and pretty. Come now, confess, you entirely agree with me.

Louise put down the heavy tray on the table, which she wheeled closer to the fire. She flexed her aching shoulders, then set out the dishes of food.

—You don't think of Jemima as clever, then? William asked, smiling: she's not exactly pretty, either. More of a *jolie laide*.

Paul smiled his lazy, goodnatured smile in return.

—I'm teaching her to be less clever and more pliant and soft. The influence of love is a remarkable thing. But as for clever tricks in bed, no, I'm not against those, not at all.

—I don't believe what you say, William protested: women

are given to us to be our helpmeets, our dear companions. We should allow them all the education they want. It can only improve them. An educated woman has something to talk about. Imagine spending your evenings being forced to converse with a boor who can chatter of nothing but knitting. No wonder so many husbands are driven from the hearth, from all hope or expectation of domestic happiness, when their wives are so incapable of sharing their thoughts or ideas in any way. You might as well have done with it and marry a cow and live in a stable.

—You really think human nature can be changed by education, don't you? asked Paul: you really think a person can be influenced by the moral and intellectual environment he is brought up in?

—I do, William replied firmly.

—I don't, Gilbert said, laughing: human capacity is fixed at birth, and there's an end to it. Agreed, a greater degree of wealth and freedom will doubtless lead to a greater measure of happiness, but the rich man's character will be as determined by nature as that of his brother crowing on a dunghill. This is the conclusion I've come to, I'm afraid.

—The Revolution should be putting all these ideas to the test, William mused: we should be experimenting with bringing up children in a different way. Teaching them the principles of the new, just society. Impressing these into them at the tenderest age.

—Removing them from their mothers, then, Paul said, laughing: it's the mothers who put all the wrong ideas into the children's heads. It's the mothers who teach girls to become little good-for-nothing nincompoops whose only thought is to trap a man and tie him down. Remove all the babies, I say! Let's set up baby factories, run on principles of reason and sanity, crèches for the *sans-culottes*, with equality printed on all the teething rings. And then, my dear William, oh yes you'll certainly see a world built on truth and justice, the end of poverty, the lion lying down with the lamb and licking her all over, till she purrs and waves her legs in the air.

—You're impossible, William said goodhumouredly.

—No, Paul said: I'm hungry and thirsty. Let's have some more wine. Look, the woman's brought in our food and we're letting it get cold. Here, have something to eat.

He speared a leg of woodcock from the plate of pieces Louise had carved for them, then pulled it apart with his fingers and stuffed it into his mouth.

—There's soup first, Louise protested: before the meat.

—I hate soup, Paul said: take it upstairs to the girls. Do them good after their ordeal, poor things.

9

After dinner the two fathers paid a visit to the new mothers upstairs. Both were still drowsy and exhausted after the births, hardly noticing what was going on around them, so the young men, shy of disturbing them, soon came clattering downstairs again, complimenting each other on their magnificent offspring. Louise, sweeping the corridor while she waited for a possible summons from Jemima or Annette, thought that both William and Paul looked relieved that they had not had to sit at their women's bedsides for too long.

William went, whistling, into the salon.

Paul, as he passed Louise, put his arm round her and kissed her cheek. She twisted away from him in surprise.

—Oh, don't be so haughty, he said: I only wanted to thank you for all you've done for Jemima. We couldn't have managed without you. You're a jewel.

—Thank you, sir, Louise said, and continued sweeping.

—You're a very pretty girl, Paul murmured: I hope you don't mind me telling you so. Intelligent, too. If I needed some more help with anything, you'd be the person to come to, wouldn't you?

He dug into his pocket then closed his fingers round Louise's hand, forcing her to let go of the broom. It clattered to the tiled floor. She opened her hand and looked at the coin gleaming on her palm. It was the equivalent of a week's wages.

—Oh, she stammered: thank you.

Paul kissed her swiftly on the mouth. He put his arms round her and held her close to him.

—Well then, my dear Louise, I shall come to you for any help I need. I'll pay you well for it, I promise. And it will be our secret, won't it? Just between you and me.

Louise wriggled free. Her knees shook. She managed to nod. Then she pocketed the coin and fled upstairs.

A little later on, she looked in on the salon. William had opened his bag and brought out a pack of cards, a box of dominoes and a chess set. The two of them were playing cards, not very seriously, and laying wagers on any absurd ideas that came into their heads.

—I'll bet you that this Revolution will be sunk and scuppered within two or three years at most, Paul offered: all your noble ideals washed down the drain in a tide of blood. Including ours if we're not careful. I think it will soon be time to get out.

William swept the cards together. He began building a tower with them, laying them on delicately, storey by toppling storey.

—We should be thinking of names for the babies, he said: I'll bet you that you won't be naming yours after Robespierre. Pierrette? No, I don't think so. Some good old-fashioned name for you.

—I suppose the births ought to be registered, Paul said.

He waved a hand at Louise, who was patiently waiting for them to notice her.

—Hey, Louise. Your mother was the midwife, wasn't she? She must know how these things are done. Tell her to come over tomorrow and we'll go to the *mairie* and fix it up.

—Yes sir, said Louise: I'll be glad to help.

—Good, Paul said: I hoped you would.

The four of them went the following day, Paul and William walking in front and Amalie and Louise coming on behind with the two tiny babies well swaddled in shawls against possible chills. You could hardly see their faces at all. Just their noses peeping out.

Outside the *mairie* a couple of decisions had hastily to be made.

—I'm going to say Jemima's my wife, Paul said to William: I don't care whether it goes against her principles or not. She must think of the child. It's getting dangerous to be an English person in Paris. If she's thinking of going back there at some point, she'll be much safer as the wife of a French citizen. Sooner or later England is bound to go to war with France, I'm certain, and then we'll see all the English rounded up and thrown into jail. There are bound to be reprisals. So Jemima now becomes Madame Gilbert. It's the only thing to do.

Louise was relieved to hear him speak so affectionately of Jemima. Yesterday she had feared he did not care deeply for her, but now his little speech reassured her that he was not unfeeling after all.

—I shall do the same, William said, after a pause for thought: it's what Annette wants and expects, after all, and it's a better start in life for the child. Later on, well, we'll just have to see.

Louise and Amalie signed the register too, as witnesses. William named his child Caroline, and Paul called his Maria.

—For Mary Wollstonecraft, he told William, laughing: Jemima insists on it. Poor little girl – what a start in life!

Afterwards, back at the house, they celebrated. Annette and Jemima got up for the occasion. They came downstairs in dressing-gowns and reclined in armchairs on either side of the blazing fire. Amalie came in, and the old caretaker, and François.

—This is nothing if not a democracy, cried Paul, waving his glass: welcome, my friends.

—A toast, William said: to Caroline, and to Mary.

—To all the heroines of the Revolution, Jemima said.

—To peace, Annette said.

Louise helped the two mothers back to bed. Amalie,

François and the caretaker went back to their various occupations. Paul and William stayed by the fire, drinking steadily. Outside it began to rain.

When Louise came in to clear away the tray of the others' dirty tumblers she thought they both seemed quite drunk. She took in their condition at a glance from their red faces and slumped bodies, their hollering laughter and slurred speech.

—Fortunes of war, dear boy, Paul was saying: surely she can't expect . . .

He was having some trouble pronouncing his words. Surely came out shurely and expect as shexpect. Suspect was shushpect.

—Shushpect, Gilbert said with a hiccup: surely she can't shushpect? These aren't normal times. She can't shexpect you to—

—I don't know what to do, William said: there are all my relatives at home, waiting for me to return and take up where I left off. This has only been a breathing space, after all.

He leaned forwards, elbows on knees, and groaned. He seemed to be addressing the fire.

—I'm a poet. That's my God-given vocation. How can I abandon my whole life's purpose? My future awaits me in England, not here. To abandon poetry would be a great sin, I'm certain of that if of nothing else in this world.

Louise went back into the kitchen. She had carried the babies downstairs in their cots, one at a time, so that they could wail in peace without disturbing their mothers. Both Annette and Jemima declared themselves exhausted and in need of sleep. The infants were ranged at a safe distance from the fireplace. They screwed up their little red faces and yelled. Louise crooned to them as she walked about trying to put the room in order. Wet nappies steamed on a rack on one side of the fire while slightly drier ones festooned the backs of chairs. The room smelled of baby urine, milk and vomit. The atmosphere was oppressive, cold as well as stuffy. The air felt damp, despite the blazing fire, as though they were underwater. Moisture seeped up from between the tiles of the floor and patterned the base of the walls.

There was yet another bucket of washing to hang up to dry. Louise looked around and considered. Then she picked it up and lugged it down the corridor to the salon.

Paul and William took no notice of her. They were still talking animatedly. She collected three chairs, set them in a row by the window, and began to drape them with wet chemises.

—That's what we all say, Paul drawled: it was an accident.

William buried his face in his hands.

—I shouldn't let anything get in the way of my poetry, he said: and children, I've observed, have a habit of doing that. How on earth shall I provide for the two of them? I've scarcely enough to live on myself, as it is.

—You can't marry her yet, in any case, Paul said: not while your two countries are probably about to go to war. You'll have to go back to England for the time being. She'll understand that.

He cast a look around the room and its draperies of steaming cloth. Louise had filled up the chair backs and begun on the table edge.

He burst out laughing.

—Come on, William. Rain or no rain, we're going out. It can hardly be wetter in the garden than in here. We need some fresh air to sober us up.

They banged out of the house, wrapped in their cloaks. Louise watched them through the window, heads down against the sheeting rain, stalk up and down the garden paths.

Later on that evening, just before Louise returned to her own home, Paul gave her a purse of money. He pinched her thigh through her dress and winked at her.

—There you are, my dear, he said: that's to thank you for all you've done for us.

She ran home, the purse hidden under her shawl. Once she was sure that her mother and sisters were asleep, she got out of bed and crept over to the fireplace. Squatting down by the glowing red embers, she tipped the contents of the purse into her palm and saw gold, rolling and shining, golden as fruits in paradise.

It was quite simple. Thanks to Paul Gilbert, she had enough money for her dowry. Her marriage to François was now secure. For that, Louise knew, she would have done anything.

Next day, William and Paul returned to Paris on their hired horses, promising all kinds of things: to return soon, to send letters, money if needed, to summon their beloved companions as soon as the two women were well enough to travel.

From Paris, William wrote to Annette to say that since all foreigners were being urged to leave Paris, and that since as an Englishman whose country was possibly about to go to war with France he felt forced to be prudent, he was reluctantly quitting her in order to return home and put his affairs in order. Annette wrote back to say that she perfectly understood, that she respected the course of action he had decided to embark upon, that she knew their separation was temporary, and that she looked forward with passionate and undying love to their reunion, whenever that might be. It could not be long. A few months at most. She knew he thought of her as his wife, she wrote, and in that spirit she signed herself always yours most devotedly.

Paul wrote to Jemima that business was taking him out of Paris to Le Havre, where a certain project of his, concerning a ship laden with cargo and destined for the Baltic, had run temporarily into trouble, so that his presence was urgently required.

—This is the first I've heard of it, Jemima exclaimed: I never knew he had anything to do with shipping at all. Why couldn't he have told me about it before? How secretive that man is.

She immediately wrote back that, being now in perfect health and strength once more, she intended to join Paul in Le Havre. She wanted him to see his baby daughter grow up, and she herself desired his company. She was setting off immediately.

—So you do really love him, then, Annette said: it was so hard for me to be sure before this, what you really felt.

—You mean because I refused to get married, Jemima replied: don't you? There is such a thing as love without marriage, you know. As you very well know.

Annette hesitated.

—You probably won't thank me for saying this. But are you sure it's wise to go haring off after him before he sends for you? He seems to me the kind of man who likes to make the decisions. Shouldn't you wait until he tells you to come?

Jemima kissed her.

—Oh Annette, I'm not like you. I'm far too impatient to sit and twiddle my thumbs until he gets round to sending for me. I'm like him. I too like to make decisions.

The two women parted as good friends. They kissed each other on both cheeks and put their arms round each other. Then Jemima, clasping the baby Maria in her arms, was gone.

10

Maître Robert, the lawyer who owned the house, turned up one day soon after Jemima's departure, to collect the rent and enquire whether she wanted to renew her tenancy for another six months. He had sent a letter announcing his arrival, so Annette was not taken unawares.

—He wants to check up on what's going on here, she said to Louise: he's heard some gossip, I expect, and he's coming to take a look for himself.

She got out of bed, and dressed, with Louise's help, in a loose, comfortable gown of grey muslin and her black shawl. She had not recovered from childbirth as swiftly as Jemima. Despite all Amalie's care, the tisanes she had prepared for her, the rest and sleep she had prescribed, she still felt very weak. Her legs wanted to crumple. The salon seemed oddly big and light and empty. Partly it was the lack of Jemima, her cries and exclamations. Partly it was the view through the window, the changed skies, scoured and whitened by the approach of winter, the trees outside half leafless now, fringed black against pewter light. At four in the afternoon there was already the threat of darkness. Annette had left the baby sleeping soundly upstairs. All baby paraphernalia had been cleared away to the kitchen. She settled herself by the fire, patted the widow's cap she had thought fit to put on, to make sure it sat neatly on her dark curls, and sighed.

Maître Robert was a big man with a face typical of the district: he had a long nose, strong cheekbones, piercing blue eyes, and a mouth that looked sulky until he smiled. He was perhaps thirty-five. He was not as thin as most of the country people. He was on the way to becoming well padded. He exuded an air of comfort and certainty.

He took to Annette immediately. She looked so young and dignified, sitting as upright as possible in her stiff-backed chair, speaking so earnestly, while her grey and black mourning clothes, however falsely assumed they might be, only made her youth all the more touching and appealing.

Louise could see that Annette was quite unaware of this. She was only anxious to persuade this hulking man that she would make a good tenant of his house for as long as he would let her take over the lease. Maître Robert did not seem unbearably surprised that a young widow with a new baby should want to live here in this small, poor village all by herself. He shrugged to himself and drank the wine, from his own cellar below, that Louise offered him. Annette had not dared tell him how much wine had been drunk during the young men's visit, and she hoped he would not find out. He had not indicated that he wished to check the contents of the house as a condition of renewing the lease. She prayed the idea would not occur to him and chattered brightly, hoping to distract his thoughts. He listened to her gravely, his calm blue eyes meeting her shining brown ones.

—In these strange times, dear madame, he said, tapping the bowl of his glass with one fleshy finger: who can know what the future holds? I myself have work that calls me away to Paris at the moment, much as I should like to avail myself of this house as my country retreat. I may, at some point, be able to escape back here from the demands of the law, but, for the time being, I am only too glad to have found such responsible tenants, first of all Madame Boote and now yourself. Shall we decide for

what period we shall make our new agreement? What would
suit you best?

Annette needed to play for time. William knew she was
here, and here she wanted to stay until any further news came
of him.

She hesitated.

—Could we say another six months to begin with? Would
that be all right?

Maître Robert smiled at her. The flesh of his face creased up
and his white teeth showed. He put his fingertips together
around the stem of his glass and nodded his head.

—Of course. With pleasure.

Annette beckoned to Louise, who came forward and poured
more wine into the lawyer's glass. His sharp bright eyes went
on studying Annette as he sipped and chatted. Louise thought
he had probably sized up the situation without a word having
been said. Young women hidden away in the countryside with
new babies and no husbands in sight might declare themselves
newly bereaved and grieving widows but there was about
Annette something so full of hope, so determinedly clinging to
life, that the lawyer could not possibly be taken in. He was
clearly sympathetic, however, and that was what mattered.

Now he was pocketing the copy of the lease and the two
months' advance rent and bowing over Annette's hand in
farewell.

—If I can be of any use to you at all, dear madam, I beg you
to feel you can rely on me. At any time.

Annette's thoughts were rather too obviously elsewhere. She
looked up in surprise.

—Oh, thank you. You're too kind.

His horse clattered away down the lane. Louise shut the tall
gate after him, then trudged back across the bleak, bare garden
and into the house. All right, William, she thought. You've got
six months' grace. Get a move on.

PART FIVE

Calais

1

Annette and the baby survived the long, hard winter, the cold spring, the world blocked by snow. It fell in the night, hush-hush on the roof as softly as rain, and when you woke in the morning you found the daylight dimmed by a thick lace screen of snow crystals. Annette went on feeding the baby herself. There was no wet-nurse available in the village, and, anyway, she liked it. She was pleased that her milk came so copiously and well. She made jokes to Louise about the cows' milk, which froze and clinked in its can and had to be knifed out, a cold white fuzz, before you could melt and heat it in a saucepan. The baby thrived, and Annette tried to ignore her chilblains, the chilliness of the house, her worries about letters from England that did not arrive. She felt that William, like the rest of the world, was imprisoned in ice. The cabbage leaves were glazed with cold, almost transparent. The apples in the store room were balls of coldness. The birds hopped forlornly from branch to branch of the white bushes outside. Washing yourself was an unattractive idea, because it meant taking off your clothes. At bedtime Annette took baby Caroline into bed with her, to make sure she did not freeze to death in the night.

Nothing was heard from Jemima either. Annette clung to her belief in William and her belief in God. Her faith kept her

going all through the winter and burst up afresh in the spring.
Even the execution of the King in January could not kill her
hopes. The snow thawed to slush. The village lanes were gul-
lies of sticky mud. And then at last it was May, with soft blue
skies and warm sun, and then June. And finally, the news came.

Annette had fetched a basin from the shelf behind the back
door then gone out to the kitchen garden plot to pick redcur-
rants. François had discovered the bushes in a corner, hidden
by weeds. Now that François had married Louise and taken
over most of the work of Amalie's farm he had no more time for
gardening. The grass waved around Annette's knees. She
struggled through a sea of green stalks, juicy and vivid after the
recent rain. At this time of year the grass grew so fast it seemed
to jump up before your very eyes, thick and feathery and soft.
She had not intended her new flowerbed to turn back into a
meadow, but it had happened. She really ought to cut it. It
would make good hay. One tiny bale, which she could give to
Louise.

Her thoughts ran, as they always did, into the channel of
her longing for William. Silently she beat her fists against his
chest, only he wasn't there, crying: why don't you come? Why
don't you send for me? You are my whole life and without you
my existence is meaningless. Why don't you come? The sad
refrain went on in her head while she crouched down by the
redcurrant bushes, put her basin on the ground, and began
swiftly stripping off the bunches of red fruit from under the
golden-green leaves. She nipped each bundle of scarlet globes
between thumb and forefinger, so that the clumps of currants
fell intact into her bowl, and none got squashed or fell off into
the long grass. Her fingers stretched out, pulled at the fruit,
picked and caught it. A soothing ritual. She felt calmer. She
talked to William more quietly now. We have a daughter, do
you remember? She too needs to see you. Does that mean
nothing? Yes, I know our two countries are now at war. So why
did you not send for me sooner?

She carried the heaped bowl back to the house. A mad-

woman, she thought: talking to a lover like a ghost. Why was
she bothering with these tasks of daily renewal, of cooking and
jelly-making and fruit-picking? Because life had to go on,
because of Caroline; and so she had to perform the jobs she had
learned from Amalie and Louise and not complain out loud,
even though her heart was torn to ribbons; because the church
taught that women suffered, and had to endure. In the kitchen
she dumped the bowl of fruit on the table, closed her eyes and
clasped her hands together and said a little prayer. Blessed
Virgin, you know what it's like. Help me find the strength to
carry on.

She picked over the fruit quickly, removing an earwig, a few
leaves, then washed it in the wooden bucket. She took the
water to the windowsill and tipped it over the flowerbed outside. She didn't bother taking a fork and stripping the fruit
from the stems. Louise had shown her it was quicker to throw
it all into the pan together, stalks and all. The stalks didn't
affect the taste one bit, and afterwards you discarded them
after you'd put the whole lot through the sieve.

The copper pan, borrowed from Amalie, was wide and deep.
Fruit and a snow of sugar heated gently together. Annette stood
over the pan with a slotted spoon, skimming off the pink scum
that frothed up in rounded clouds, as the surface of the red
mass began to heave and boil. She dipped her spoon down-
wards, tucked it under the plump cushions of airy pinkness
that bloomed above the red of the seething fruit, caught the
foam, whisked it aside and shook it into the saucer she had
placed ready at the side of the fire. She kept on stirring, moving
her long spoon gently between the sodden sunk globes of currants, easing them up from the bottom lest they catch and burn.

The fruit had to cook for the space of one decade of the
rosary, a string of Aves of boiling sweetness, a delicious perfume
both sugary and sharp. The steam composed itself into
William's face and she felt comforted.

She hefted the pan off the stove, mashed the hot juice and
pulp through a sieve, also borrowed from Amalie, then ladled it

into pots. Clear scarlet jelly shone back at her. She felt pleased with herself. She had created something. She had made something happen. She might be riven with sorrow but she was capable. She set the pots on a tray and carried them out into the cool, dark shed where they kept all the preserves.

When she came inside again Louise was standing in the kitchen, untying the strings of her cloak, two overflowing baskets on the floor beside her. She looked breathless and excited. As soon as she saw Annette she dived her hand into one of the baskets and drew out a letter.

—It's from William, she said.

Annette fell into the chair beside the table and burst into tears of angry relief.

—Why did it take him so long?

She scanned the letter, then looked up, puzzled.

—He's not coming here. He wants me to meet him in Calais, and he suggests I leave Caroline behind. He's bringing his sister Polly with him. How odd.

—Then you should take me with you, Louise said: two against one isn't fair. François will agree, I'm sure. He won't mind my coming with you.

—Don't be ridiculous, Annette said: you're making it sound like a battle.

A loud cry came from upstairs. Caroline had wakened from her nap. Annette jumped from her chair and ran to her, hastily wiping the tears from her cheeks so that the baby should not see them and be upset.

2

Annette began sewing a new dress for Caroline, in order to show her off to best effect to her father. She had kept all her old dresses from the period she considered her girlhood, which was over now. She had decided to exist in a kind of permanent widowhood and dressed in sober greys and dark blues and black, colours which in fact suited her very well, bringing out the freshness of her complexion and the gleam of her hair. She went into her bedroom and knelt in front of the cloth-covered trunk she had placed at the end of her bed and used as an ottoman. She lifted off the clothes she had tossed there earlier that day, piled them to one side, then eased back the heavy lid.

She was not prepared for the pain that struck her like a clenched fist to the belly. Here was her life with William, brief as it had been, folded and tidied away, smelling faintly of the lavender sachets placed between the folds. The cream-coloured boots she had worn that first night of meeting him. The pink jacket and sash, the sprigged linen gown, there they were, neatly rolled up so that the material would not crease and crack. There too were the pale blue silk gown with the white lace fichu which she had worn for the evening parties at her friends' house. Plain, simple clothes, in the new style that had been just coming in. Here was a dress striped in pink and rose, with a knot of pink ribbon on each shoulder. She had worn that the day she and William walked along the river, under the poplars, when they sat down on a bench and kissed each other. Then they had sneaked into his rooms, choosing their moment carefully, when his landlady was asleep after her dinner, and waiting until she went off to evening mass to slip out again. Five hours in bed together. It had been five minutes and five months, the warmth and play, the sudden stirring of desire, then the throb and pulse between her legs that demanded she go on, and on, and become satisfied. Over and over they had found out how to please each other, giggling into the pillows like two conspirators, rolling over fighting like two cats, rocking and cradling each other. After that she had gone back as often as she could, in search of the renewal of delight.

She scooped up the flowered linen dress, the pale blue silk one, and the striped one, and cast them on the floor beside her. She picked out the pink sash, and a blue one. She shut the lid on the rest. Time enough to let Caroline rootle through them and choose what suited her once she was older. For the time being, these relics would do.

Downstairs she cleared the kitchen table, laid her heap of brightly coloured dresses upon it, and fetched her sewing shears. She cut up her life with William. She unpicked its seams and ripped it apart in her haste. She tore out stitches and slashed skirts into pieces. Then she stitched all the bits back together again. She re-made her life on a smaller scale. To a new pattern. This time, for Caroline. A tiny version of herself, who would look charming arrayed in this *bergère* frock panelled and gathered in bands of sprigged cream linen and rosy stripes, with a small lace fichu and loose sleeves.

For herself she permitted the smallest of hopes to dawn. She cut up the blue silk evening dress and made a new lining with it for her cloak, and she used the leftover pieces to make a couple of silk roses which she stitched on to her little straw hat. Her gloves and shoes were shabby, but she had no money with which to replace them. Her parents, once the baby was born, had assumed that William had taken over paying maintenance, and sent her just a token amount of pocket money each month. Annette was too proud to tell them the truth. She pawned her jewellery and took in sewing to pay the rent and Louise's wages.

Louise packed a basket of provisions for the first leg of the journey. They would have to eat in the inns where they changed horses, but at least they could save money at the start. She put in a loaf of bread, a lump of cheese, some dried sausage, and a packet of dried apple rings threaded on a string. Everything was well wrapped up in cloths, to keep out damp, flies, fleas and any other hazards they might meet with on the road. Since they did not know what the weather would be like when they reached Calais, they wore their warmest underclothes and outerwear, reckoning that they could always shed a layer or two if the far side of Normandy was not as windswept, cold and rain-sodden as they had always been led to suppose.

—Why do we have to go so far to meet him? Louise grumbled: you'd have thought he could have made a bit more effort and come a bit further this way.

Annette defended him.

—How can we tell? All I know is that he is bringing his sister Polly with him and her health may be fragile. Also, he says, they cannot stay long, because of certain responsibilities back home, and because of the war. He will only be allowed to stay for a couple of days. Better to have more time to spend with us in Calais than to waste it journeying all the way down to Saintange and back.

Louise was not quite satisfied. She was bothered about something. It nagged away at her. Better spit it out, she thought.

—Why are you taking Caroline with you? When he expressly told you not to?

Annette laughed.

—Oh, these men, they think they're no good with children, but I know he will love her the instant he sees her again. She's his daughter. He can't not want her to come too. And she's weaned. She'll be no trouble.

Louise tried to put it as gently as possible.

—You don't want to put his back up. I know how desperately you want him to recognise her, to accept her as his daughter, but—

Annette turned on her in a fury.

—How dare you talk like that! He is coming to make amends to me, we will make plans, we will work out how to create a future together, don't you dare talk to me of leaving our daughter behind! She must begin to get to know him now, before we are married. Then, when we go to live with him in England, she will not be nervous, she will only look forward to seeing him again.

Louise went in tucking the cloths round the provisions in the basket. Having relieved her mind of its burden, as far as she dared, she felt calm. I've done my best, she thought. Well, not my complete best, I don't dare, that would be impossible, but at least I've said something. Now it's up to her, poor thing.

Annette folded her arms and looked unseeingly down at her woollen mittens.

—He'll make a settlement to tide us over, while the arrangements for the marriage are completed. There'll be some money coming regularly. At last.

—Thank God for that, Louise said. To herself she said: but, Annette, if he didn't say so in the letter, how do you know?

She put the basket near the door, along with the wicker hamper that contained a change of clothes for all three of them.

The journey to Calais was slow and uncomfortable but Annette didn't mind it. She kept Caroline amused as best she could with caresses and songs and games of pat-a-cake, she chattered to the other passengers, she dozed when Louise took her turn to hold the child.

On arrival in Calais they took rooms in the centre of town, dumped their baggage, and then immediately made for the beach. It was the first time either of them had seen the sea. It was a wild, windy day. Their hair whipped out from under their hats, blew about their faces and stung their eyes. Their skirts billowed and ballooned as they struggled over the damp stones. The sea, capped with white fringes, tore up to them then retreated. It advanced and pawed and bucked, like a huge green bullock charging you to knock you down. The wetness in the air clung to them and deposited itself on their tongues. Caroline screamed with delight, clinging on to her mother's neck. Annette embraced the sea with her eyes, straining to make out any sign of the packet boat which was not due till tomorrow as she very well knew.

Their landlady cooked them mussels for dinner, which they washed down with tumblers of cider. Next came stewed apricots and a piece of cake. That night they slept soundly, sharing a bed to save money, with Caroline laid across the bottom, at their feet, like a fat little bolster, wedged in by pillows.

In the morning Annette went for an early walk down on the beach, to try and calm herself. Caroline danced up and down at the window in Louise's arms, waving at gulls. Her smile broke out broadly when she saw her mother coming back. A welcoming babble broke from her lips, like the cry of the gulls.

William's instructions in his letter had been precise. Annette was to book rooms for himself and Polly in some cheap but respectable lodging house near to their own. The packet was due in at ten o'clock. They would all meet at the Customs House, then Annette would show him and Polly to their rooms, leave them to wash and unpack, and join them for dinner a little later on.

Annette read out these directions for the tenth time.

—He's thought of everything, she said.

—I certainly hope so, Louise replied.

One thing he had not thought of was that Annette might disobey one of his orders and bring their child with her, and

Louise too. As he stepped on to the quayside his face changed from surprise to disapproval. By his side Polly grinned from under the hood of her cloak which the wind flapped about. She was tall and thin, with piercing green eyes and a lot of black hair that the wind was undoing and sending tumbling about her face.

—Well, Polly cried: I certainly didn't expect this.

She swooped down on the child and tried to kiss her. Caroline burst into tears and hid her face on her mother's shoulder. Annette jiggled her and soothed her. Louise busied herself fetching a porter and a barrow and supervising the loading up of the visitors' bags. They were surrounded by the commotion of the landing: passengers exclaiming and calling, luggage being unloaded and piled up haphazardly on the quay, children darting about. Overhead the gulls wheeled and screamed and cats fought over pieces of salvaged fish.

The bags were taken into the Customs House, cleared by the Customs official and then released. They set off, an eccentric little procession, into town, the two tall thin English people with their distinctive and shabby clothes, the two Frenchwomen. Bringing up the rear came the porter, a cheerful man in a blue blouse who perched Caroline on the top of the barrow, wedged in among the bags.

—Such a very lively smell, Polly exclaimed: of fish!

—The smell is all right, Annette assured her: once we get away from the jetty. In a moment you won't notice it at all.

It was odd to hear Polly speak French. She looked so wild and so foreign you expected her to speak gibberish or to caw like a crow. But though her accent was most peculiar, Louise could just about understand what she said. She had been learning French specially for this visit, Polly told them, so they felt they had to be grateful.

—How are you, Annette? William asked: I hope you've been well.

Louise could see Annette trying hard not to weep at the sight of him, so longed-for, so distant, and so absent, and now

suddenly here, walking along a narrow cobbled street at her
side. His face was as gentle and kindly as ever. Perhaps he had
more of a worried and serious air. Louise, trotting along beside
Polly, slowed her pace, to give William and Annette the chance
to outstrip them and talk to each other privately. But Polly took
no notice of this ploy. She chattered and laughed, especially to
her brother. She called to him constantly.

Louise and Annette ended up eating their dinner together
without the other two, as William had developed a violent
headache after the rough crossing and its bouts of nausea and
vomiting, and had had to take to his bed. His landlady promised him hot bricks and tisanes and bowls of broth, and Polly
insisted on sitting with him, so there was nothing for Louise
and Annette to do but to withdraw. Not having ordered dinner
at their own lodgings, they went to a seafood stall near the
jetty, where a man and his wife were serving up fried fillets of
cod. Upended barrels served as tables, planks on piled boxes as
benches. The woman poured them cups of cider from a jug,
and the man dropped their pieces of cod into sizzling oil. They
ate the fried morsels of fish with relish and fed mashed-up titbits to Caroline. They did not speak of the visitors. They
discussed the food, the view, the weather. They wiped their
smelly fingers on their pocket handkerchiefs. Then they went
down to the beach. The wind had dropped and they both felt
like staying outside.

Annette settled herself in a comfortable spot just below the
sea wall, a large boulder at her back. She draped her red kerchief over her head and shoulders, to protect her skin from the
sun, and took the sleepy Caroline on her lap. Louise sat down
to divest herself of boots and stockings then picked her way
down over the stones towards the water.

The tide was going out. A band of shingle glittered in the
sunlight. Beyond it was an expanse of shining grey sand,
shaped into curves and ripples by the waves that had passed
over it. Louise ran to the edge of the sea and planted her feet
in the delicious cold that lapped her ankles and made her tingle

all over. She longed to pull up her skirts between her legs as
she had seen the fisherwomen do up on the jetty, but she didn't
quite dare. So she looped them up over her arm like a tail. She
splashed along the tideline, toes curling into the wet sand,
enjoying the tug on her soles each time a small wave broke over
her feet and raced backwards again. The retreating sea had
flung up a belt of broken shells, dead starfish, driftwood.
Louise hopped about, examining these, then ran back into the
water splashing herself as high as she could.

She made her way steadily along the beach towards the
cliffs that backed its right-hand side. From time to time, to
begin with, she turned round and glanced along to spot
Annette, who would wave to her. Then, as she grew more
absorbed in the pleasure of walking alongside the sea, she
looked back less often. This walking made Louise very happy.
Just the simple motion of going steadily along, putting one
foot rhythmically in front of another, set up currents of bliss
inside her, as though the sea were in her heart, pushing
through her whole body, while the light dissolved her and
drew her into itself. She was enveloped in heat and happiness; her wet skirts clinging to her legs felt weightless; she felt
like singing aloud.

She reached the cliffs, then turned. It was now mid-
afternoon. Earlier on, she had had the beach to herself, strolling
in a vast deserted landscape of sand and sky separated by a strip
of greeny-blue sea. Now, Louise saw that the sunshine had
tempted out another little group, who were pacing towards her,
very slowly, from the other end of the beach. A tall man and
woman, and a small woman with a bright red kerchief just like
Annette's.

It was Annette, carrying Caroline. Walking with William and
Polly.

She hesitated, unsure whether or not to approach them. But
then Annette waved, so Louise went forwards slowly. She felt
unwilling to relinquish her free time, her solitude. She didn't
want to take Caroline and amuse her. She didn't want to have

to deal with these English people and their tricksy behaviour. She didn't want Annette to be upset.

It was too late to wish that. Even at this distance she could see the rigidity in Annette's body, the over-polite way she turned her head to her companions. Of course I'm fine, her gestures said: look how perfectly in control of myself I am, you won't catch *me* howling like an animal, certainly not.

As Louise came up, Polly gave a piercing whistle. She had her fingers to her pursed lips and was screeching like an emergency siren. She laughed triumphantly at Caroline.

—I bet you didn't know grown-up ladies could do that!

Caroline screamed. Annette ran forward and thrust her into Louise's arms.

—Please will you take her, just for a bit? She's had too much sun and she's over-tired. Take her back to the lodgings and I'll join you there in a little while. Please. I'll come soon.

William had been crying. His eyes were red and swollen. Seeing Louise glance at him he produced a large blue handkerchief and began energetically blowing his nose. That was the last time she ever saw him, weeping and stricken on the beach at Calais, while Polly giggled and Annette stood white and helpless with shock, her hands grasping the silk-covered button that fastened the flap of her little bag, tearing at it so violently that it twisted off and fell into the sand.

Later on the two of them talked in low voices, crouched over the driftwood fire the landlady had lit for them in their tiny sitting room. Next door, Caroline slept. They kept the door half open so that they could hear her if she woke up and cried.

William's announcement was a simple one. He had travelled to France to tell Annette of his forthcoming marriage to an old friend of Jemima's, a young woman called Fanny Skynner, whom apparently he had known for some time, and with whom he had an understanding, reached before he left for Paris the previous year. Polly had met Fanny, apparently, and liked her.

—That's it? Louise asked disbelievingly: that's all?

—It's obvious, isn't it, Annette said: Polly has come to guard him, to make sure he gets away from me and really does marry this Fanny. She's his dragon, always at his side. Poor William, to feel so weak. I think perhaps he'll find it's Polly he's marrying, not Fanny at all!

Louise searched for words of comfort.

—Well at least he came and told you himself, rather than just writing a letter. I suppose that's something.

—That makes him slightly less of a coward, yes, Annette agreed: and he did only manage to do it with that terrible Polly standing next to him, oh yes, he managed it all really well. What a hero.

She smashed her fist against her palm.

—Anyway, my dear, first thing tomorrow, as soon as it's light, you and I are off by the early coach. I've got to get away as fast as possible. I'd go now if I could. I can't bear the thought that William might try and see me again. Ever. I've got to get away.

She did not cry then, nor in the night. They lay side by side, sleepless, Annette as still as stone, Louise more restless, turning from side to side. They did not speak. They waited for the light to pierce the crack between the shutters and announce the new day and their release from this room which was too small to contain so much grief.

All the way home Annette kept her own counsel, and Louise approved, for what was there to say? You couldn't discuss your broken heart on a public coach, especially not with a baby jumping up and down in your lap and needing to be stopped from fretting. Annette's eyes looked strange, somewhat wild and staring, but she spoke gently to the child, and politely to the other passengers, and from time to time she took hold of Louise's hand and held it in an impersonal kind of way.

What would I have done? Louise thought: if I had lost François like that? She couldn't imagine. When they reached the village and she had seen Annette back to her house she hurried to her own home. Here she considerably surprised François with the warmth of her greeting, not caring who was passing the farm and might see her casting her arms around him outside in the yard.

The following day Annette got up because she had to. Caroline needed her. There was work to do. Otherwise she thought she might have tried to snuff herself out somehow, like a candle that's guttering down and the kindest thing you can do for it is to extinguish it. She dragged herself about the house, performing her tasks as though she were a clockwork toy. She said to her hands pick that up, or stir that gruel, or change that nappy, and they obeyed. She felt distant, as though she'd been stunned. Some damage had been done to her, which rendered her incapable of feeling much. It was better that way, because if she did feel anything she thought she might break into pieces. At the end of the day, she put herself to bed. She lay in the darkness and said to herself: there, you did it. Now do the same tomorrow and then for a million more days and then you'll be dead and quite safe.

Maître Robert came on a second visit, to collect the rent and once again to renegotiate the lease, which had run out two months ago.

—Legally speaking, Maître Robert said: I'm afraid you shouldn't be here at all. Pardon me, dear madame. My little joke.

Annette attempted a listless smile.

—We'll pack up and go immediately, she said: I'm sorry, I'm afraid I had no idea – I completely forgot . . .

Her voice tailed off and she looked down at her hands. Maître Robert hurried to make his little speech. He did not want her in his house as a tenant, he explained, because he would so much rather she inhabited it as his wife. Would she do him the honour of accepting his proposal?

Annette would. Hardship had taught her the value of having a practical approach to life and not rejecting the windfalls, like husbands, which fell into your lap. Her soul cried out that she was selling herself for respectability and her calculating mind replied that it was a bit late to start worrying about that, she had to feed herself and her child. She explained all this to Louise in the kitchen later on, and received in turn a compliment on her good sense.

Now Louise came in with the decanter and glasses on a tray just in time to see Maître Robert kiss Annette's hand.

—I'll do my best to make you a good wife, she said, and burst into tears.

PART SIX

Saintange-sur-Seine

1

Louise thought of the years that followed as the time when they all kept their heads well down and concentrated on surviving. The Revolution gathered momentum like a great wave, smashed over them in the tides of blood that were the Terror, then ebbed again. From these convulsions the new France was born. Death throes or labour pangs: Louise had not been quite sure what she was witnessing. She foresaw that within her lifetime the lot of people like herself would not dramatically improve. She had prophesied this even before the deaths on the guillotine of the King and Queen. She did not repine. She simply got on with what had to be done. Work, work, and more work. She bore three children, and buried one of them. Amalie died. She melted away at the end of winter, like the snow. For a while, Louise felt that she had gone down into the grave with her mother, and then she discovered that Amalie lived on inside her. She heard her voice quite distinctly as she went about the house and garden, chiding, instructing, joking, complaining. This was a gift she could not ever have dreamed of receiving, for no one had told her it was possible. Amalie was dead, certainly, but she was also risen, like Jesus, and had come back to live with Louise. It was a great comfort, for which Louise thanked God. It made her understand religion better.

On the other hand, although the churches had opened up again, she did not bother going to Sunday mass. She reasoned she had no need. Also, to a certain extent, she wanted to stay out of God's way. She didn't want to remind him, or herself come to that, of what she'd done, the crime she'd committed in order to get money. The God she met outside church, in the fields, seemed less of a judge, less frightening. She said her prayers to that God, and hoped for the best.

Annette lived quietly with her husband and daughter. Maître Robert's legal practice took him occasionally to Paris, and sometimes he asked Annette to accompany him. She shook her head and said no. Throughout the Terror she remained a staunch Royalist and Catholic who made no secret of her sympathies, and she wanted to run no risks. She was safe in the village. She stayed at home and gave Caroline her lessons. When she had completed all her household tasks for the day, she would take Caroline upstairs into her bedroom, close the door, and teach her English for an hour or so. Maître Robert believed that these were courses of catechism she was giving her daughter, as befitted a good Catholic mother, and did not interfere. He dutifully acknowledged the Supreme Being who blessed the Revolution, but he let his wife pray as she wished.

—But why should I learn English? Caroline sometimes complained: we're at war with the English. They're our enemies.

Annette did not offer convincing explanations at these moments. She would say vaguely: one day, you never know, you might want to read some English poetry.

Caroline was tall and thin, olive-skinned, with blue-green eyes. Her hair was like her mother's, thick and dark, but she had not inherited her mother's curls. She was delighted when Annette allowed her to cut her hair short in one of the Greek crops that had been fashionable for a while. Doing her hair in the mornings was now just a matter of running her fingers through her mass of feathery tufts. Then she was off outside, to play with the dogs or climb the big apple tree in the corner of the garden. Annette had forbidden her to mix with the village people and their children. Caroline assumed this was for reasons of simple snobbishness, and shrugged. Louise knew better. Annette did not want Caroline overhearing anyone's reminiscences about certain male visitors, so long ago.

—It's for her own good, Annette told Maître Robert: she's grown up thinking of you as her father, and that's the way I want it to be. You've been a good father to her. She couldn't have had a better. Let sleeping dogs lie.

There came a time, however, when the dogs woke up and barked loudly, when Maître Robert showed his teeth and snarled and howled.

Things began to go wrong in November 1809, when Caroline was seventeen. Annette surprised everybody, most of all herself, by becoming pregnant. She assumed, when her periods stopped, that she was entering the change of life. A little early perhaps, but that was the way it was. Both her parents had been dead for some years, so she could not ask her mother for advice. She turned to Louise instead. Louise dropped in most days, to keep an eye on things and have a chat. The two women were good friends, even though these days Annette sensed a certain reserve, a certain distance, in Louise. She puzzled about it for a while, then concluded that marriage, and all the cares of raising a family and helping to run a farm, meant that Louise had less time for intimacy than formerly. Louise was happy to let her think that that was the reason. When consulted by Annette about her symptoms of dizziness and nausea, Louise stood stock still with shock as the truth dawned on her. Then she said: tell your husband he's going to be a father at last.

—A father *again*, Annette said.

Annette fell ill in the following spring with what seemed just a feverish cold. She moved about the house on trembling legs, leaning on the backs of chairs for support. Her weakness and malaise were exacerbated by her pregnancy. She felt sick most of the time and vomited often, much more than she had done when pregnant with Caroline. She grew so thin that her belly full of baby looked no bigger than a ball. Finally, at her husband's worried insistence, she took to her bed.

—I'm much too old to be having a child, she complained to Louise: people will laugh at me, if they aren't doing so already. Caroline's nearly grown-up. It's ridiculous.

Louise was kneeling by the bedroom stove, stocking it with fresh wood. It was small, and had to be fed with stout sticks rather than logs. If you forgot to check it and put more wood on, it went out after half an hour. Annette shivered, even under her heaped quilts, so Louise had taken to coming round two or three times a day, to see to the stove. Caroline often forgot.

—Think how happy it's making your husband, Louise offered: men are always happy when their wives are going to have a baby.

—Poor man, Annette said: he's had to wait a long time.

She turned her head on the pillow and summoned Louise with her eyes. Louise rose, dusted her hands on her apron and came over to the bed. She sat down on the chair beside it and took Annette's hand in her own.

—Should I tell Caroline the whole story, do you think? Annette asked: sooner or later she might find out anyway. Don't you think it would be better if it came from me?

Alarm leaped up in Louise and clutched her by the throat.

—Oh no, I shouldn't think so, she replied: and who else is there to tell her, anyway? Both your parents are dead, your two brothers have gone abroad, and people here in the village don't know anything for certain. Who is there left? Only me. And your husband, of course. *He* won't tell her.

Annette's face was pale. Her little aquiline nose jutted out from her sunken cheeks. She looked like a woman of over fifty not of thirty-six. She lowered her eyes and contemplated the folded-back edge of the sheet. She spoke with effort, as though her words had teeth and hurt her mouth.

—There's William. One day he might want to see her. He might send for her. Then she's bound to ask me, why didn't I tell her before?

Louise squeezed Annette's hand so tightly she made her wince.

—If he wants to send for her, he will. But it's unlikely, isn't it? He hasn't done so up till now. If he doesn't want to see his daughter, well then, he doesn't. You must respect his wishes on that. I think it's much too late to tell her now.

—He asks after her in letters, Annette said: the few times a letter's got through. He never forgets. Polly always puts a note in too. Her French is quite good now. She went on learning it specially so that she could write to me.

—You've told me that before, Louise said: stop talking so much. It tires you.

Annette looked towards the little cabinet which stood on the left of the fireplace. It had curly legs and was painted with wreaths of flowers.

—When I'm a little stronger I'll get William's letters out again. I like to look at them.

Louise released her hand. She stood up, bent over the bed, plumped up the pillows. She stroked Annette's forehead.

—Stop thinking about the past. You've got to think about the future and the baby now. Caroline is all right. She's a fine strong girl. You've no need to worry about her. Save your strength for yourself.

She did not believe these pieces of advice she delivered with such brisk cheerfulness. She administered them to Annette as the doctor administered leeches and cupping. Because that was what one did in crises. If you admitted you did not know what to say or do then you were done for. Louise could see perfectly well that the doctor had no idea of how to cure Annette of her fever and her excessive vomiting and no idea of telling her so. He administered his treatments and medicines, pocketed his fee, and departed. Louise lied to Annette just like Maître Robert and the doctor did. They assured her that she would get well soon and then she would be able to recover her strength for the approaching birth. They repeated this like a prayer.

Maître Robert came into the bedroom carrying a glass containing a nosegay from the garden. It was the signal for Louise to depart. She closed the door quietly behind her and went downstairs. Once inside the kitchen she sank down on to a chair by the table and covered her face with her hands.

—Don't die, she said to the darkness behind her eyes: I don't want you to die.

Then she busied herself heating up the broth she had brought over for Annette. It calmed her to have something to do.

At dinnertime Caroline ate heartily. She had been outside, playing with her spaniel, for most of the morning, and she looked rosy and bright-eyed, invigorated by the exercise. People called her a pretty girl, and Louise, watching her shake out her table-napkin and smile at Maître Robert, thought they were right.

—I'll go and sit with Maman this afternoon, Caroline offered to her father: she gets lonely on her own for too long.

He grunted his assent. He was tearing through his lamb cutlets as fast as was consonant with manners and dignity while reading some legal document he had placed beside his plate. He had his reading glasses on and from time to time he wiped them with his handkerchief when they steamed up from the hot food.

—Oh, I shouldn't disturb her, Louise said, passing Caroline the platter of potatoes: she needs to sleep. Leave her in peace for a little while. Why don't you get on with the mending? There's an enormous pile of it waiting to be done and God knows I haven't got time.

Caroline was supposed to be learning how to keep house, now that her mother was ill. In the interests of economy Maître Robert preferred to keep just two servants, young women from the village who came in to labour away at the scrubbing and heavy cleaning and who took the washing off to the *lavoir*. Louise helped out as the occasion arose. Annette had done all the cooking and the lighter housework herself, had looked after

the poultry and tended the vegetable garden. Caroline had not
realised how much work it entailed, keeping even their small
household going. Louise had to nag her to get her to help. Now
she was groaning in exaggerated and theatrical fashion, trying
to lighten her father's mood.

—I loathe sewing. I wish we were back in the Garden of
Eden wearing fig leaves. No darning ever.

Maître Robert grunted again. He covered his mouth with his
napkin and spat out a piece of bone. He moved his hand in the
air and Louise stepped forward to hand him the dish of stewed
onions. Later on, leaving Caroline grumbling over the sewing
basket by the kitchen fire, she tiptoed upstairs to see if Annette
was in need of anything. When she peeped round the bedroom door she saw Maître Robert seated by the bed. He was
redfaced and crying. Annette was asleep.

2

Annette was too weak and enfeebled, when her labour pains began two weeks early, to go through with giving birth. She died and the baby too. The doctor did not get a chance to show off his skill with forceps, and for that everyone was grateful.

The baby was inside Annette and Annette was inside the coffin. François made it for her, using some planks of cherry wood from the tree in the garden. Maître Robert had been keeping the wood, once the tree was so old that it had been cut down, to season, to make a cupboard with, or perhaps a bed, to give to Caroline when she married. But now with the wood François made the coffin. Annette would fuse with the tree. She would rot into the ground like the tree's bruised fruit. They all stood around the grave as the coffin was lowered in and said the last prayers, and then came back to the house for a glass of wine and some cheese pastries. Caroline ran about with the tray, serving her father's relatives whom they saw rarely. His sister, his brother, with their spouses and children, stood glumly by the fire in the salon. The food and drink got them through the awkward hour. Then Caroline drove the children out into the garden and started them running races up and down the paths. She joined in the running herself, until she was exhausted, the blood drumming in her head and her knees aching, her calves in shock after striking the hard ground.

Louise crept upstairs, into Annette's room. She stripped the bed, in which the body had lain for the customary three days, until yesterday, and heaved the quilt across the sill, to air. Then she opened the little curly-legged cabinet and took out the thin packet of letters she found on the bottom shelf. She unpicked the knot of the blue ribbon that bound them, and opened them up. There were just two of them. She glanced at them, to make sure they were the right ones. Almost illegible squiggles met her eyes. She peered closer at the crabbed black hand that wrote one way, filled the page and then criss-crossed it the other way. She couldn't understand a word, which meant the language must be English. She saw the names Polly and William, which convinced her. She thrust the letters into her apron pocket and took them downstairs with her into the kitchen where she burned them in the stove. Then she went into the garden, kissed Caroline goodnight, and went home. She had the milking to do and her own children to feed.

3

Night-times were like the house: dark, enveloping. Since having the children, Louise slept lightly. Part of her stayed on the alert, ears cocked for the crying or restlessness that meant possible illness. When they were babies who needed feeding at night, she took them back with her into her own bed. François slept holding the covers wrapped about himself as though someone might steal them, his face, in the dawn light filtering in, rapt and concentrated as he dreamed. He was far off, yet he was close. She would push her feet against his back and gently prop herself against the wall of him, settling the baby to her breast, the three of them breathing all together like one milky animal.

Now that the children were older, aged fifteen and thirteen, they slept in the big bed in the far corner. Sometimes they had nightmares and woke whimpering, but mostly they slept like François did, as though they'd been flung down from a great height, stunned into unconsciousness. Louise remained the lightest sleeper of them all. Tired out though she was every night she stayed awake for an hour or two, resting in a space carved out of blackness that was hers alone. She thought about the children and how to keep them alive, about what work needed to be done next day, about their debts. Sometimes her mind cleared of all these worries and she just lay awake in the darkness, not thinking at all, floating peacefully on a sea that held and cradled her, that rolled her back and forth, rocked her up and down. Then the sea became Amalie, and then sleep would take her down to its depths and she would know nothing until the cock was crowing and the dog barking and the room was pierced by shafts of early morning light.

If the dog barked in the middle of the night it meant that something was wrong. The owls were quiet. It was the dog she heard. He started then stopped. A growl, a burst of yapping, then silence. Louise sat up, on the alert. A fox, perhaps. Or it could be an intruder. But the dog was quiet again. She yawned, lay back down and fell asleep.

This year the plum tree bore more fruit than ever before. The weight of it weighed the long, slender branches down to the ground, where they vanished in the grass and got tangled together with convolvulus in wild bouquets. Louise had no time to spare for fancy gardening. She cut the grass for hay in June and that was that. This year, because of the heat and the wet, the grass had grown up again, thick with flowering weeds. She picked some clover and wild geraniums and put them in a jar on the kitchen table. Then she took two baskets and returned to the orchard to pick the plums. She did this late morning, after the dew had dried off the plums and they would not spoil, and before it got too hot. It was the last couple of days in the month when it was still possible to pick fruit, before the moon began growing again.

The plums were so ripe that they fell into her hands. They smelled fragrant in the warm sunlight, as though she were biting them off the tree and tasting their sweet juice. Flies rose up in clouds as she pushed into the web of branches and she beat them away from her face in clouds. They had got there first, settling, in blue glints with jewelled wings, on minute cracks in the fruit that oozed gold. The plums were purple with a dusky bloom, almost pink in places. Those that were not perfectly ripe were tinged golden-green. She worked steadily, cupping her hand around each heavy little fruit, taking it with her fingers; just a slight pull; then her hand closed on the loose plum and she dropped it into the basket at her feet. Rapidly she repeated this gesture, over and over again, marvelling at the number and size of the thick clusters. In twenty minutes her two baskets were piled high. She licked juice off her fingers and stood up straight, bracing herself for the walk with the heavy load back to the house.

—Louise! Louise!

It was François' voice, calling her. Startled, she almost dropped her freight of plums. The baskets tipped as she jerked with surprise, and a few plums rolled along the dusty path. François rarely raised his voice to shout like that. At the very least it must be an adder in one of the sheds, or an accident. François was not afraid of adders; he simply killed them. Therefore one of the children must have got hurt. Might be bleeding. Might die. She stood unable to move, while words formed in her brain: don't let them be dead, dear God, don't let them be dead.

François' voice came again. This time she heard extra words and felt less frightened.

—Louise, come here. It's Madame Annette's girl. Come quick. Help me.

The outhouse where François found Caroline was a cave in the side of the hill against which the house was built. They used it as a shed for storing odd baskets and buckets which went nowhere else. The shed had no door. You could run in and out of it quickly to fetch a container for potatoes or cabbages. It was a place Louise did not like going into because grass-snakes lived at the back of it. She shuddered to see Caroline there.

The girl was lying curled up tight as an autumn leaf, rigid as a baby who does not want to be born. Her head was hidden in her arms and her fists were clenched on either side of her face. She must have crept in here because there was no door and she could easily get in and hide. But why hide at all? Why not rouse them if she needed them?

—She must have been there all night, Louise said: that must have been why the dog began to bark. He heard her come in. Of course he knows her. She would have quieted him.

She bent over the girl who lay, locked into herself, on the hard ground. She touched her hair. The girl jerked and moaned.

—Caroline, it's me, Louise. We're going to take you into the house. Come along now.

Between them they lugged the young woman to her feet. Now she had started to weep. She kept her head down, her fingers clasped over her face. They took an elbow each and steered her across the yard. She stumbled up the steps of the house and fell into the darkness inside.

—We'll put her in our bed, Louise said: and get her warm.

She didn't know why she said this, except that she felt she bore in her arms a small wounded animal, and when you found one you cradled it to see how badly hurt it was, whether it was dying or would have to be killed, whether it could be revived in any way.

Caroline had no shoes on. They tipped her into the unmade bed and drew the clothes up over her. Louise called to her son who was hovering with his sister over by the door.

—Go on with your work outside and don't come back until dinnertime. Go on, go away. Do as I tell you.

Caroline was shivering and gasping. Louise did the simplest thing. She drew her feet out of her sabots, got into the bed, which was still warm from the night before, and took Caroline into her arms as you would a fractious child, to contain and soothe its thrashing limbs. At first Caroline hardly seemed to know her, and cried and struggled. Then, as Louise held her firmly and talked to her, she calmed down. Her tears soaked into Louise's bodice.

—Tell me what it is, Louise repeated: tell me what's wrong.

François went over to the door.

—I've got to get back to work. I'll see you later.

The latch rattled and banged behind him.

Caroline shivered. She put her face against Louise's shoulder and sobbed it out.

—My stepfather. He's not my father at all. He told me he's my stepfather. He said I was another man's bastard.

Louise could feel Caroline's warm snot and tears dripping down her neck. She tightened her hold on the girl and rocked her hopelessly to and fro. Dear God, she thought: so now what shall I do with her, poor thing? She's going to suffer all over again if she finds out more of the truth.

—There there, she crooned to the girl whimpering in her arms: there there.

She made a rapid decision. Tell Caroline only as much as she needs to know. Keep everything else as dark as possible. Don't let her find out too much. It will only hurt her.

She mopped Caroline's face with her sleeve.

—Come on now. There's my girl. It's all right. I'm here.

Too late. She was lying. It was not all right, but she could not admit that.

—I'll make you some breakfast, she said: that will put some strength back into you.

She wrested more of the story out of Caroline. She sat on the edge of the bed and spooned chestnut porridge between Caroline's lips as though she were still a baby, and in return got spits and dribbles of words. It took half an hour to feed her and make sense of what she said, and it was time Louise could ill spare from her work. She kept at it, saying: and then? and so?

After the funeral Caroline had gone home with the man she thought of as her father. His brother and sister had stayed one night and then left. The rain kept Caroline indoors. Grief for her mother, as she described it, stung her eyes like sleeplessness. She felt herself ping like a wire, as though she might break. She was empty and scoured out. To fill up the fragile-walled space inside her, she sorted through her mother's things, while her father sat downstairs in the dining room and stared out of the window. He was allowing himself three days off for mourning. After that the tide of clients, papers, seals, would roll over his head once more. Caroline left him alone because that was the message conveyed by his back and profile: go away. She crept into the room where her mother had lain, and touched the coverlet of the bed, the padded top of the prie-dieu. She traced the edge of the chest of drawers with her fingertip, weighed her mother's rosary in the palm of her hand, coiled up, a crystal snake.

The letters were in a packet pushed right to the back of the top shelf, behind rolled stockings. They were tied up with green ribbon. Her mother had explained that to her as a child: green, the colour of the early days of the Revolution, the colour of hope. Caroline untied the letters and read them. There were five of them. Three were from a man called William Saygood.

—He's my father, Caroline said: why was I not told?

The two other letters were from a woman called Polly, William's sister, written in careful, schoolroom French. Both writers referred to the child with obvious affection. Both spoke to Annette with esteem and respect. The woman Polly had sent her little notes at Christmas. She called them: my annual chat with you, our little bit of gossip. Annette had obviously not kept all of the letters. Perhaps she had felt she had to destroy some and keep just a few as mementoes. Perhaps she had decided it was both dangerous and useless to dwell on the past. How could Caroline know? She could not ask Annette to tell her the truth now, because Annette was dead and buried and could not come back. And when she confronted Maître Robert, he had lost control, in his grief, and screamed at her that indeed she was not his child.

Now Caroline did cry. Now that it was safe to do so, now that she would not break apart into little pieces shattered on the floor, all the parts of herself so scattered and destroyed that she would never get mended again. She cried now because she knew that she would have to be stopped, because Louise could not spend all morning listening to her; she was a busy woman with a great deal to do, and she would have to staunch Caroline's tears with her usual briskness and common sense;

there, that is enough now; just as she would scold the soup when it rose and frothed in the pan and she snatched it off the stove. So Caroline wept her due length of time and then gulped and blew her nose. She climbed out of the bed, went outside and pissed behind the barn, came back in and washed her hands and face. Then she sat at the table with Louise, sorting through the heap of plums, and discussing what to do next.

—You can't go and see him just like that, Louise objected: you can't just turn up on his doorstep. You must write first, and tell him of your mother's death, and see whether or not he wants you to visit him. In any case, he might have moved. How do you know he's still living at the same address? And how on earth will you get to England? Who'll pay for it? Where's the money coming from? And how can you possibly travel on your own? There's a war on, don't forget.

Caroline repeated: I've got to find my father. I've got to know who he is.

—Of course Annette never thought you'd find out, Louise said: she never wanted you to be hurt, of course not.

Caroline was busy blowing her nose.

—Then she should have destroyed all the evidence, she said: and covered her tracks. How could she imagine I wouldn't discover those letters some time? She took a stupid risk keeping them and not even hiding them very well.

Louise stood up, wiping her hands on her apron.

—She did what she thought was best, she said: for herself and for you. You can't ask for more than that. I realise you're very upset, but you must not speak rudely about your mother. You don't know what she had to go through.

—That's her own fault, Caroline said: she didn't tell me.

Louise shrugged.

—Well. I've got to get on with my work. You stay there for a bit and rest, and I'll see you home at dinnertime.

4

—You must go home, Louise insisted: as though nothing has happened. Don't let him know you were out all night. It's enough to make him have you locked up. You must stay on your best behaviour. Then you'll be able to seize your chance, when the time comes.

—It may come sooner than you think, Caroline told her.

—Go and pick a marrow from the vegetable garden, Louise instructed her: you can say you came up here to get some vegetables to cook for dinner. And I'll walk you back, because I'm coming to collect the washing, to give the servant a hand. That way he won't wonder what I'm doing in the house.

Maître Robert was in his study at the far end of the corridor from the kitchen. Louise began cutting up the marrow while Caroline ran upstairs. The little packet was where she had left it. She opened the creased pages and flattened them out. With a stub of pencil she scrawled William's address on a scrap of paper. Then she replaced the packet of letters in the cabinet and ran lightly back downstairs.

The soup was quick to make. Marrow slices tossed in butter and crumbled sage leaves, simmered in stock and a little milk. Caroline laid the table while Louise went about the house fetching the dirty linen which she tied into a huge bundle

inside a sheet, knotting the corners across like a bunch of ears.
She felt they looked so normal, and yet their little world had
changed and could never be the same again. It was like another
convulsion of revolution, an upheaval strewing rocks and boulders in its wake.

Caroline curtsied to Maître Robert as she always did, then
they both sat down, unfolded their napkins and spread them on
their laps. Louise, sorting the heap of cloths she had dumped
on the tiled floor just outside the open door, peeped through
the crack and listened to their polite chat.

—Were you ill this morning, Caroline? enquired Maître
Robert: I couldn't understand it, you didn't come downstairs to
make breakfast. I had to make do with cold water and a piece
of fruit. I do hope you are not going to give way to some
malady. You must be strong, my dear, and not succumb to your
emotions.

He nodded his head at her in what he clearly intended to be
a kindly way. Perhaps he regretted his outburst of the day
before. Caroline looked down at her hands. She spoke in a cool
little voice.

—I was unwell this morning, so I stayed in bed. But I'm
feeling much better now.

—Good, said her stepfather.

He lifted the lid of the tureen and ladled some soup into
Caroline's plate.

—Eat something, then. You must keep up your strength.

Louise outside could have laughed at how meek Caroline's
voice was, thanking him. But she knew her too well. That
sweet little girl's voice masked something much angrier and
more determined. It spelt trouble.

Caroline, in giving certain instructions to Louise, had relied
on the fact that her stepfather would not re-enter, for some
time, the room where the corpse of his wife had lain. He would
not imagine he needed to check its contents and protect them
against thieves. Louise hurried in and took the smallest, most
portable things out of the little cabinet: the silver thimble, the

gold medallion of the Virgin, the earrings and bracelet, the miniature portrait of Mr Saygood. They were Caroline's anyway, she argued with herself, or at any rate they ought to be. So there was no harm in removing them just to make sure they did not get given away to someone else, to Maître Robert's sister or niece for example. She thrust them inside a pillowcase which she then carried downstairs with the rest of the dirty washing.

—Don't try and sell them until you're far away from here, she advised Caroline later: perhaps not until you're arrived in England.

—I've got to go to Paris on business for a few days, Maître Robert was telling Caroline: will you be all right by yourself, or shall I send you to my sister's house?

He fished critically with his spoon.

—What kind of soup is this supposed to be?

—Marrow, Caroline replied: Louise has a glut of them in her garden and we thought it was time to use them up.

Her stepfather put down his soup and dabbed his lips with his napkin.

—Too spicy for me. I don't like pepper, as you surely must know by this time.

Louise wondered why they could not mention Annette. She supposed that each of them was too proud to admit that the other might have a right to feel some grief. She did not know how much this man had loved her friend. She did not know anything any more. Presumably he had wished for children. The pretty young woman he had married, in what must have been a fit of gallantry and desire, had given him none, all those years. Did he resent her for that? He must have wanted a son, Louise thought, because all men did. Had he secretly resented all along the fact that Annette had had a lover?

There they were, the two of them, passing the bread and discussing whether or not the butter the marrow had been sautéd in was not a little rancid, with Annette buried only two days ago. Caroline had brushed her hair; she had put on a clean kerchief and splashed her eyes and face with cold water to subdue the signs of crying. She had removed all trace of the wild girl of the early morning. Her stepfather, too, was cold and composed. Well, Caroline was acting. A useful skill if you planned to leave home without permission.

Louise put her head round the half-open door.

—I'll be off then. I've got the washing.

5

To his daughter Caroline, William Saygood was insubstantial as a dream. Like a dream, his image exercised its power over her even while she was fully awake. She thought about him all the time. Reveries concerning him rushed to fill up any gaps in the day.

She tried to explain it to Louise. How she didn't know the simplest things that made him who he was. Whether he put milk in his coffee or preferred it in potent black thimblefuls, whether he ever wore a red cravat, whether he wrote at night or by day or both, whether he could whistle, whether he felt bored and depressed on Sunday afternoons.

Caroline could not touch him, because he was not there. She could not learn the way he laughed, or smell his damp coat in the rain, or discover whether the palm of his hand, placed flat against hers, was hard or soft. Her lack of him was a place she flowed into. She outlined what was missing, then coloured it in. His absence was a shape solid with her curiosity.

One of her games now was to invent him. She compiled a clutter of pictures of fathers from the meagre sources to hand: the black and white cartoons that decorated the newspapers; the stained-glass windows in church; the miniatures pinned up in her mother's bedroom. The fathers were like the dismembered dolls of her childhood: she shifted faces and limbs around as the whim took her, when she was dissatisfied with one version and wanted another. To a golden crown and a silver sword she might add a gun for shooting rabbits and a poacher's hat, a pair of white leather shoes with high red heels, a fishing-net, a flute. Sometimes William languished in prison, accused of Royalist sympathies and condemned to the guillotine, and Caroline visited him, smuggling him a file hidden in a loaf of bread. Sometimes William had wings and flew. Sometimes he rode a black stallion and galloped towards her across beetling black crags. Often he lay in a flowery meadow by the side of a lake in England and wrote poems.

It was this unknown place that drew her towards it.

She stitched Annette's jewellery, and the money she had filched from her purse, into a belt that she buckled around her waist under her chemise. It chafed slightly and made her itch but she didn't mind the discomfort. It was a constant reminder of her purpose and it made her feel somehow safe, contained, to be encircled by the thick strip of linen. She couldn't spill out, she explained to Louise.

The two notes from Polly spoke of the north of England as a place of mists and fogs, torrential downpours, snow and ice. There did not seem to be any mention of summer when she scanned the letters again. She decided she would have to dress accordingly, in her thickest boots, a woollen jacket, a woollen overcoat. She tucked Polly's letters into her deep inside pocket, so that she could produce them as proof that she was indeed who she said she was. She wrapped the miniature in her spare handkerchief and stowed it away in the same pocket. William's address she had off by heart.

She waited until her stepfather had left for Paris. She left him a note saying that she had decided to go and stay with a childhood friend of Annette's in Blois.

Leaving home was one of the simplest actions she had ever performed. She walked out of the house and locked the door behind her, put the key under a stone, walked across the garden and out of the gate on to the lane, locked the gate behind her and placed the key under another stone, walked out of the village. Half an hour later she was on the public coach, heading for the coast and for England.

Louise, who had helped Caroline with her preparations and received all her confidences, now fell ill. Something struck her down. She thought perhaps it was the fist of God, punishing her for what she had done. She slumped in her chair, shivering and miserable. She missed Annette. She wished she could talk to her, and try to explain. Since that was impossible, she finally decided to send for the priest.

PART SEVEN

St Paul's Churchyard

1

Jemima Boote sat in the small parlour of her attic lodgings over Mr Jackson's print shop in St Paul's Churchyard and listened to the rain outside. It had been raining on the day she first moved in, eighteen years ago, to the rooms which Mr Jackson was in the habit of letting cheaply to friends in need and which, on the strength of Miss Wollstonecraft's recommendation, he had agreed to let to her. Neither of them had expected the arrangement to last so long. But here she still was, glimpsing herself now as she had been then, desperate, distraught with grief, her world breaking up in pieces around her, trying not to cry as she stood on the doorstep wet through and listened to the bolts being worked open from the inside. Mr Jackson had apologised, in his brusque way, for the poverty of the accommodation, but to Jemima, blundering in from the rain, it had been shelter enough. All she had wanted, that day, was somewhere to hide, a safe place in which to lie low and lick her wounds.

Now she was warm, because she had a good fire, and had stopped up, with bolsters, the draughts whistling under the badly fitting door. She was dry, because Mr Jackson had finally had the roof mended. She was comfortable, because she had bought herself some new cushions to pad her little armchair, which was drawn up close to the hearth. She had her writing-desk on her knees and a cup of tea on the table nearby. Her cat sprawled, a tabby puddle, at her feet.

She was supposed to be completing the third volume of her latest novel, for she had a deadline to meet and was behind with it, but she could not settle to working out the next flourish in her fantastical and improbable plot. Her thoughts kept sliding away from her work to her memories of eighteen years before. The words she meant to scratch down shrivelled then vanished. The ink on her nib shrank and dried.

Just so had Annette Villon faded then gone. The *faire-part* from Maître Robert to William, which William had forwarded on to her with a brief note, had arrived as a great shock. Annette was dead. Annette was buried. That was the translation of the formal florid words engraved in flowing copperplate. Death. The word chopped at you like an axe.

Jemima had assumed that one day, when the war between their countries was over, they would be able to meet. She had cried all morning at the knowledge that Annette was gone – *dead* – and that she would never see her again.

After that first, brief acquaintance, Jemima had gone on thinking of Annette as a friend. She had heard from William that Annette had married the lawyer who was her landlord, that she and Caroline were well, that they had survived the Terror and avoided the fate dealt out to those who remained Royalist and Catholic, who supported the rebel priests who refused to take the Convention oath of loyalty to the state. But she had not written to Annette. Her excuse to herself had been that letters might not get through because of the war, but the truth was much more shameful. The real reason had been her pride. She could not bear to talk about what had happened to her. She could not bear that Annette should know and should pity her. She had begged William never to mention the tragedy, and she was sure he had kept his promise. He too did not want to dwell on the sadness of the past, on what might have been, he scrawled in reply to her letter. His letters to France were few and brief. It was better that way. Better too, if the letters had to pass through a censor's hands, to say as little as possible about anything that mattered.

True friendship, Jemima thought now, meant telling each other things; sharing secrets when necessary; witnessing each other's lives. You held the memory of each other, the events and changes. You knew what the other person had been like as a girl. Before marriage closed round her and veiled her. You saw that girl go on. But she had not done that for Annette. She had let her slip away and lose contact. Jemima had promised herself that one day she would write a long letter to Annette and tell her everything that had happened and ask her pardon for having been so stiff-necked. Now it was too late.

Jemima sipped her tea and twirled her pen between her fingers. She could not concentrate on her writing. The adventures of her heroine, locked in the skeleton-filled dungeon of the wicked count's castle on an island of the Venetian lagoon, had ceased to interest her. The image of Annette filled her mind, a gentle ghost who glided into the room and smiled. How often she had dreamed of Annette visiting her one day. Now she never would. It was her own fault. Her own stupidity.

The candles on the mantelpiece, stuck in yellow porcelain holders decorated with pink butterflies, were guttering down. Jemima sat in a pool of tremulous and glowing light. Beyond her chair, shadows lay thick in the corners and along the dark red walls. The shutters were painted amber. Jemima liked these colours, which remained pleasing even though faded. Mr Jackson let her the rooms furnished, but she had brought in a few extra things: the armchair and table, the writing-desk. The candlesticks were hers, the two green wineglasses, the teacup and saucer. She had crockery and cutlery for two people, just enough that if Mr Jackson or some other friend dropped in for dinner or supper, she could manage. She had imagined sitting here in front of the fire with Annette, talking and arguing. She had wanted to show her friend St Paul's, and the river, and all her favourite haunts in the City. Now that could never happen.

What would become of Caroline? Maître Robert would expect her, Jemima supposed, to stay at home, a good and dutiful daughter keeping house for him, until she married. Probably it was all mapped out. Perhaps there was already some young man waiting in the wings.

Caroline was eighteen. Jemima's own daughter, had she lived, would have been exactly that age. Not a day passed in which Jemima did not think of little Maria, buried in the cemetery at Le Havre. Over and over, day after day, the relentless details presented themselves: her flight after Paul to Le Havre, the jogging discomfort of the public coach, the baby in her arms wailing with what seemed like violent colic, her panic at discovering Paul nowhere, the inn in the docks where she finally put up, from whose front window you could see the great ships sailing out to the open sea. The doctor had said that nothing could be done and that it was not Jemima's fault. She hadn't believed him. The horror of the child's death from convulsions, her tiny body arched in agony, could not be erased from her mind. She felt that she laid herself in the grave with the infant. The ardent, hopeful, desiring woman in love pulled the earth over her head, and went down into the underworld.

—You must have strength, madame, the doctor said: you are still young. Life goes on.

That was the worst of it, that it did. With both Paul and little Maria wrenched from her, utterly vanished, one dead and the other too desperate to get away from her to be able to tell her so, Jemima found herself alive and alone. She forced herself to go on. She became a brisk, hardworking journalist who kept herself by writing articles and Gothic novels. Her dream of writing a book about the Revolution had long since withered away. Others did it, and did it better than she could ever have done. She had been sure of that ever since those days in Saintange-sur-Seine, when she had sat in her room pretending to write a political memoir and scribbling a romance in secret instead. She had discovered that she wanted to tell stories. She gave her heroines more adventures than she had had herself, but less misfortune. Her ambition to become a great writer had vanished. She had survived, and that was sufficient. If she could scribble her novels, well and good. If she could earn her own living, and be a nuisance to no one, she was content.

She had reached the point, after eighteen years of bitter grief, of being able to think of Maria with the most tender sorrow and regret. Of Paul she thought occasionally, with mild curiosity. She could accept, now, his need for headlong flight away from her and their daughter. It was over. It was so long ago. It wasn't that I wanted him to marry me, she had imagined writing to Annette: I despised that institution for the enslavement of women, as you very well know, and as I thought he did too. But he didn't believe me. He thought all women secretly longed to be wives, however apparently independent we were. He could not imagine that I loved him yet did not want to take money from him.

In the event, she had not been able to live up to her own principles. She had let Paul give her money towards the rent of the house in Saintange, and towards the expense of caring for the baby, before he left, and she had agreed to him registering the child in his own name, as though he and she were married. She had put her ideals aside, and been practical.

Sometimes, on evenings like this, when she thought of the past, she felt lonely. Tonight, with Annette's death so fresh in her mind, she was not lonely so much as filled with sadness all over again for what was lost. As she so often did when she was by herself, she summoned the image of her dead daughter and spoke to her as though she were still alive. As though she were eighteen years old, and could be told stories about times gone by.

She wanted to tell Maria about her father, the man she herself had known and understood so little. It was through Paul, after all, and his friendship with William, that she had come into contact with Annette. She had plunged into intimacy with both of them, rapidly revealing herself, as though she knew she did not have much time for the normal preliminaries of friendship.

—You have to try and understand, Jemima addressed the hovering vision of her daughter: Paris in early 1792, just before you were conceived, was a place of such violent and rapid change, such exhilaration and terror all mixed up, such pleasure and such fear living side by side, that a normal life, such as we had all been used to, was out of the question. Old ways of behaving were suspended. We had to invent new ones. When you knew that you might be picked up and flung into prison at any moment, well, at least if you feared that that might happen, whether or not such fears were groundless or reasonable, well then, you did not think too much about the future. Tomorrow was as far as most of us went.

Tomorrow was the word that she and Paul had used with each other. Until tomorrow, then. Walking and talking until all hours, back and forth over the bridges, their feet propelled by the charm and urgency of their conversations. What did they talk about? Everything. Their childhoods, politics, books, the other foreigners in Paris. They gossiped and relished and discussed. Zigzagging across the grey-green river then back again. Until it was so late, dawn light beginning to glimmer in the sky, that they had reluctantly to part. Until tomorrow, then, Jemima would say, and Paul would answer: until tomorrow. They would stroll, arm in arm, to the door of her lodgings, and part there. Paul always saw her home, insisting that the streets were dangerous for a woman on her own. Jemima laughed at him but gave in. It meant they had more time together.

One late evening, meaning to part as usual, they got trapped in St-Germain. A brawl had broken out in front of a food shop, where a crowd of furious women was denouncing the proprietor for hoarding supplies. Voices were shouting abuse, fists swinging, lanterns swaying and rocking sending light tossing over white faces, mouths open yelling. Paul and Jemima dodged away from the protesters, whose mood was ugly now, down a side street. The other end was blocked by another shouting crowd. Paul seized Jemima by the arm and dragged her into a shadowy doorway. The door behind them yielded, propelled them into a narrow hallway. Paul was addressing the woman who sat there, giving her money. Then he was taking Jemima upstairs. He left her sitting panting with shock on the hard wooden chair by the bed and vanished. He reappeared with a carafe of wine, two tumblers, a plate containing some cold sausage and a heel of cheese, and some bread.

Eating and drinking made Jemima feel better. She accepted that she would not be able to get home that night. There was no parting until tomorrow. There was this night. There was now. She stepped with eagerness into Paul's embrace. In that small hotel room in St-Germain they lay down together in the short, uncomfortable bed and became lovers, while outside the crowd shouted and there was the sound of blows, the trampling of feet, a window breaking, and finally silence except for their breathing and the creak of the bed.

She had meant to be wary. She was curious about what making love was like. She had wanted to find out. She had chosen well, she thought, a friendly man whom she liked and who was humorous and teasing. She was sure he had brought other women here, to this small, plain hotel whose chief charm was its discretion, its anonymity. It was surprisingly clean. No bugs squirmed in the bed, no fleas hopped on the floor. There was a screen in one corner behind which you could get undressed and squat over the chamberpot. That first morning, Jemima lay in the cramped little bed, Paul's head on her shoulder, and waited patiently for him to wake. She wanted to remember every second of the night just past. She studied the grey flaking paint on the shutters, the brilliant light that burned between them as though the new day were an animal desperate to leap inside and join them, she noted the smell of the woollen blanket and the smell of Paul's skin and hair, her fingers felt the bones in his forearms, she learned the rhythm of his heartbeat. She opened herself up to all these things, wanting to contain them, but she discovered soon enough that she could not control them, they entered her and took her over. Making love that morning, when Paul awoke, was less awkward

than the night before. The pain and the blood were washed
away, and in their place was excitement and tenderness.

They walked out of the hotel hungry and in search of breakfast. Women were scrubbing their doorsteps, sending streams
of water sluicing down the street. Sunlight washed the façades
of houses. The door and shutters of the food shop had been
wrenched down and smashed to bits. The inside of the shop
gaped empty, and there were bloodstains on the pavement just
outside. Paul and Jemima hurried away, towards the river.

Almost immediately things began to go wrong. Jemima
made the mistake of telling Paul she loved him. He reacted
coolly, not coming near her for a week. Remembering her conversations with Miss Wollstonecraft, she tried not to be needy,
to be strong and independent. Paul loved the idea of free
women, because he believed they did not need him. He loved
Jemima as she was at the beginning, when he could not be
sure of her, when she would tease him and occasionally turn
away. She learned that for him to enjoy her company, he had to
feel rejected some of the time. That made him feel safe. When
she discovered she was pregnant, she waited as long as possible
before telling him, fearing his response.

In fact he had been utterly charmed. He said it suited her,
being pregnant. They made love often, as urgently as they had
ever done. They built a fantasy together in which they went to
live in America in a radical commune in Kentucky.

The room was almost in complete darkness. The candles
were out. Jemima, nodding off to sleep, was roused back to
consciousness by the sound of the bell tinkling downstairs. She
got up, smoothed down her hair and her skirts, and went to the
door, yawning, blinking back tears, wondering who her visitor
could possibly be.

PART EIGHT

Greydale

1

What were they going to have for dinner? Beans, Daisy supposed. Beans to bulk out the small bit of mutton she had coaxed out of the butcher on credit yesterday. It was lying on a plate in the larder and would go off very soon unless she cooked it. A large dish of beans and potatoes, with a piece of mutton on top. They should be grateful to have meat of any description to eat at all, their bill at the butcher's was so large. It had not been paid in weeks, and the butcher was threatening to give them no more credit. So far, Daisy had successfully pleaded the cause of the four growing children, who must be fed. Her story was wearing thin, she knew. After all, the butcher had children of his own to feed. If William couldn't pay his bill, then he was feeding his own children at the butcher's expense. This might well, therefore, be the last chunk of meat they saw for a while. That being so, Daisy was determined to make a feast of it.

She fetched two baskets from the outhouse, and a garden fork, then made her way to the strip of vegetable plot at the far end of the little orchard. William and Polly, wrapped in their cloaks, were reclining on the grass, their backs propped against the gnarled trunks of an apple tree. Their heads were bent towards each other and they were talking vigorously. They stopped when she got close enough to hear, and waited for her to go past before resuming again. Offended, Daisy went to the furthest end of the two rows of beans, to demonstrate her lack of interest in eavesdropping. She began to pick, working as fast as possible. Other people might have time to lie about as languid as creatures of leisure but she had the dinner to make, the children to round up, the kitchen to clean, and a great basket of mending to see to.

She worked her way slowly along the row of plants, stooping to collect the long beans in the palm of her hand then pull them upwards against the stalk to release them. After a while she straightened up, to ease her aching back, letting the heavy basket drop down plump on to the long grass. She put her hands one on each side of her waist, massaging it, the fingers finding and soothing the dull pain. She pushed her shoulders as far back as they would go, then yawned.

Now her eyes looked outward. She saw La Colombe afresh, built in, small and square, under the high hill. William had insisted on giving his house a French name. Daisy did not know why. The beauty of the surroundings could hide from her for days, while she lugged split logs about or tired herself out weeding or tried to part the fighting children. Perhaps she needed not to see it for a time. Because then, when she raised her eyes unexpectedly and saw the place almost by chance, it would rush on her; the mountains swooped and the clouds danced; the hills and fields were grey-green-blue; she had no words for the mix of colours; it fell upon her and overcame her. The landscape was so big and she just a dot in its greenness. Such moments did not stay. They went off and she was left with her eyes wide open, looking at and really seeing the detail of white-painted window frames, the jagged scarlet line of a ragged robin blooming under the hedgerow, the purple-brown gleam, rich as butter, of the turned clay in the field, the flash of sunlight on the lake in the distance.

Such moments made it possible to carry on. They were gifts the world gave her. To join her to it again, to make her part of it once more, when she had been resisting and dreaming of running away and doing she did not know what.

She leaned into her work again. The beans dangled in clusters hidden under their leaves. She had to search for them. Bend, stoop, peer. Sweat ran down her back and face while flies from the cattle grazing in the next field swooped around her and bit as much of her exposed skin as they could manage. She tried squatting, to be closer to the beans trailing in loops and bunches along the ground, but very quickly her thighs began to ache. She pushed the basket along in front of her with one toe. She wiped her streaming face on her rolled-up sleeve and swatted the flies off with one hand.

She crept back down between the rows, relishing the earthy green scent even as she cursed to herself, feeling so hot, the blood all rushed to her face from bending so much, her fingers smarting from contact with occasional nettles. Polly was the official gardener but she did not like weeding and did not bother to do too much. She ran a hoe down once a month and that was that. She had too much other work to do, she would claim, sighing, to be able to attend properly to the vegetable garden. Four children to help care for, the plain sewing, most of the cooking, looking after Fanny. Daisy did the cleaning, the washing, the preparing and preserving of vegetables. Between them, they scrambled through.

—But she can't possibly stay with us for long. For one thing, there's nowhere for her to sleep, and for another, we can't afford to feed her. Can't you write and tell her not to come?

Polly sounded agitated. Her voice was sharp and high. William sounded more resigned.

—It's too late. She wrote that she was taking the packet on the fifteenth. She'll be in the country by now. She'll be here any day.

Daisy realised that she was closer to her employers than she had imagined. She rose and stretched, then grasped her large basket, overflowing with beans, by the handle, and laboured away with it out of the orchard towards the kitchen.

She yawned. Freddy, the baby, had been fretful all night. He was teething and she had had to walk him up and down, rub his sore gums with her finger, until worn out, he had fallen asleep on her shoulder. All the children woke at six and had to be attended to immediately, so that they did not rouse their parents. Fanny liked to be brought her breakfast at ten o'clock or so. By that time Daisy was usually so exhausted that she could have tumbled back into bed. Fat chance of that. And then William and Polly both often slept until noon. They liked to stay up late. Their admiration of nature took them out on long moonlit walks. Or else William was composing while Polly waited up for him to come in from the garden and dictate to her the lines forming in his head. Late at night was one of the few times they could talk to each other undisturbed, without the children running in or Fanny growing fretful. Sometimes Daisy in a wakeful state heard their voices in the garden below. Sliding over to the window and opening it a crack, she would listen. They talked about God, politics, the grandeur of the universe, their love for each other, William's poetry, Polly's observations of the scenery all around them. They babbled like twin brooks. She would grow tired of listening to them long before they finished, and would return to bed, with their voices dancing around each other, dancing her to sleep.

Damn. She had forgotten the potatoes. She dumped the basket of beans on the kitchen table and returned to the orchard where she had left her fork leaning against the stone wall. William and Polly were still there, hunched and miserable, like two black crows. The potato patch was quite close to them. Daisy smiled in their direction, to let them know she was aware they had seen her, and applied herself to digging. Carefully, she loosened her buried treasures. They rolled out of the soil, pale and pure, and she bent down and picked them up one by one. Her hair under her cap was soaked with sweat. She wiped a grimy hand across her face, bundled the potatoes into her apron which she held in front of her like a bag, and went back towards the house.

—Make the best of it.

William's voice floated after her, disconsolate. Make the best of what? She hadn't time to find out.

When she hollered for the three children they came running from their game in the field. Bribing them with slices of bread and jam, she set them to topping and tailing the beans and peeling the potatoes while she put the mutton into a saucepan with an onion and a prayer and set it to cook. Then she seized a broom and began to sweep the floor. It got filthy several times a day, no matter how often it was swept. The ancient flags seeped muddy moisture in winter, dust in summer. Ants ran about in the cracks, which always seemed deep in crumbs, bits of dropped vegetable peelings, goodness knows what else. Their greasy sheen begged: scrub me, but Daisy ignored it. She was behindhand enough as it was. She began swatting the cloud of flies buzzing back and forth making dives at the cooking pot. Flies got into the room because the back door had to be kept open to let in some air. They crawled on you and bit you and the bites ached and stung. The sweat that ran down you felt like flies creeping under your clothes. The only relief was to rub the bites till you broke the skin and let blood. Then they stopped itching so badly. Daisy's face and forearms were pockmarked with scars.

The children were squabbling over their task because it was so boring.

—I'm working faster than you, Anny complained to her sister and brother.

—Women's work, said Sam with disgust: I should think you ought to know how to do it.

They both turned on Milly, the youngest.

—Here, get a move on. You've done hardly any at all.

They swept a heap of beans over to her. Sam flicked a wet curl of potato peel at her, which caught her nose and hung there, absurd. The other two burst out laughing. Milly burst into tears.

Fanny came into the kitchen through the back door, closing

it behind her with a sharp clack! and waving her hands at the dense net of flies circling her head.

—Can't you keep these children quiet? she asked: William's trying to do some work. He *must* have peace and quiet.

—No, he's not, Daisy said: he's out in the orchard, talking to Miss Polly. I saw them there just now.

Fanny dropped into a chair. She wiped her hand wearily across her face, picked up a handful of beans and began pinching off their tips.

—The drain outside the privy is really stinking, she said in her faint, high voice: you must do something about it. In this weather the smell is quite unbearable. I could hardly bear to be in there, it was so terrible.

Daisy understood her anger at having to talk of such things at all. She squashed down the first retort that sprang to her lips and searched for a calmer one.

—Short of digging up the drain and moving it somewhere else, ma'am, I don't really know what we can do.

Fanny sighed. She was so little and so thin you expected to hear her bones rattle. Her face was worn into grooves of fretting discontent. Milly, still sobbing, clambered on to her knee. The other two, taking advantage of their mother's arrival, slunk over to the door and vanished. Daisy was quite sure they had gone to poke about in the drain, but she could not be bothered to stop them. It was quieter without them. At least, since the weather was unusually benign this summer, they could be shoved out of doors to play. In winter, when all of them were cooped up together inside for weeks in the kitchen, to leave William the parlour for writing in, the noise of fighting and crying became unbearable. Daisy resorted to quick slaps round the face to hush the children, but it didn't really work. It just made them cry harder. Fanny would take to her bed and forbid anyone to come upstairs and disturb her. Polly's method was based on her belief that children *ought* to be happy. When the noise of their crying reached her in the parlour, where she sat with William, copying out his poems

into a fair manuscript for the printers, she would erupt, shouting that they were wretched and miserable creatures; she
would grab them by the ear, haul them over to the cellar, push
them inside and bolt the door. This way, she explained to
Daisy, the children learned that crying did not in fact lead
them anywhere. They got no attention, and learned that
crying was not tolerated. Thus happiness was the preferable
state. An hour in the dark, beetle-infested cellar soon taught
them their lesson.

Fanny finished the beans fast, her delicate fingers working
nimbly. She swept the discarded green bits into the bucket by
the back door, disturbing the haze of fruit flies that hovered
over it. Then she got up.

—I'll go and sit in the cool somewhere, I think. My
headache is no better. It's too stuffy in here. I can't bear it.

Daisy followed her out. She carried the bucket of green
waste over to the compost heap. Then she walked down to the
stream to rinse it out. William and Polly were just coming out of
the orchard. Fanny met them. They stood in an awkward
group, a triangle that looked as though it wanted to discon-
nect, reform itself into two sharp angles with space between.
William was the apex. The two women swivelled to follow him
whichever way he faced.

He and Polly were telling Fanny something. Daisy saw her
clutch her shawl more tightly to her. She let out a wail.

—Oh no. I can't bear it.

The baby started to cry. Parked in his wicker cradle on the
garden path, he had spent the morning gazing at clouds racing
across the sky, green tendrils of honeysuckle waving overhead.
Now, his cry informed Daisy's alert ears, he was bored and
hungry and his gums had started to hurt again and he was going
to bawl until the discomfort stopped.

Daisy started walking down the path towards him, thinking
she'd scoop him up and take him inside and give him a crust to
chew on, some nice piece of stale bread. Fanny, Polly and
William, talking earnestly, were approaching from the orchard.

The three younger children ran whooping round the side of the house.

All of them were so intent and involved that they did not at first hear the faint voice calling them.

—It'll be a beggar, Daisy said: I'll go and see what he wants.

She was resigned. Beggars were frequent hereabouts. People forced out of their homes, without work, wretched and broken-down, each with a tale of distress and hardship. It was the policy of the house to give them a cup of water and a piece of bread if they asked for it, a penny or two if there was any money from the housekeeping to spare. Then they were moved on. Daisy hoisted the crying Freddy to face her shoulder so that she could pat him on the back, and walked down to the gate.

The young man who leaned there, apparently exhausted, was dusty and sweat-streaked. His heavy overcoat hung open over a thick jacket. What ridiculous clothes to be wearing in this heat, Daisy thought, looking at the boy's cheeks flushed red, the moustache of moisture on his top lip, the hair, dark with perspiration, plastered to his forehead. His hat was of velvet, a sort of floppy cap, quite unsuitable for this weather. But then, Daisy supposed, if you had to carry all your clothes with you, it made sense to wear as many of them as possible. The boy looked very young, and frightened. Daisy gave him a penny fished out of her apron pocket and told him sternly to be off.

Freddy was a warm, squirming bundle in her arms. She walked back up the path, jiggling him, then carried him inside.

The darkness and coolness inside the house fell on them, surprising Freddy so much that his bawling ceased and she was able to ferret about and find him a piece of stale biscuit. She shoved it at him and he took it happily. She meant to take him back outside, but raised voices in the passageway made her pause. She didn't want to walk into a quarrel between William and Fanny. Their voices clashed like fire-irons falling over. Then William's feet thundered up the uncarpeted wooden stairs and Fanny burst into the kitchen, sobbing. Her son, frightened by the noise, started crying too. He choked amidst his sobs on a crumb and Daisy had to bang his back to get it up again. Then he vomited on her shoulder. Fanny's wails competed with his.

—He's going off to visit the Wordsworths at Grasmere. When he knows I'm not well and I can't manage the children on my own and I've got another of my headaches. Oh, it's not fair. He never thinks of me. Only of himself. I'm worn out. I can't stand it.

—How long's he going for? Daisy asked.

—A week at least, Fanny sobbed: oh why is everybody so unkind to me?

Feet tramped to and fro on the floorboards of the room above. William, packing a bag, Daisy supposed. One of the problems of this house was the way you could always hear what everybody else was up to. She was privy to most conversations, all arguments that involved raised voices. Polly's whispers were as bad as shouts. The bed in the room upstairs creaked loudly, so that she always knew, whether she wanted to or not, when William and Fanny were being amorous. In fact Fanny made out that William was amorous and she merely dutiful. She did not want another child, or at least not soon. Gazing at her, while these thoughts went quickly through her head, Daisy understood the reason for her employer's fit of nerves. Fanny was pregnant again.

She sat down on the nearest chair, gripping the crying baby.

—Oh dear, she said: you poor thing.

Was that the reason William was escaping to see his friends? It might be. From time to time he exploded and shouted that he was being driven to distraction, that he couldn't stand, not for a single moment longer, the atmosphere of crying babies, wet nappies, stifling domesticity in general and his complaining womenfolk in particular. He would clap his hat to his head and put on his stout walking boots, shove a piece of cold meat and bread into his coat pocket, and vanish up over the mountain.

Sometimes he came back at nightfall, his frustration walked away and a new poem forming in his head. He would make his peace with Fanny and send her, kissed and fondled, to bed, then sit in the parlour, talking peaceably to Polly or just lounging next to her in easy silence. Daisy, carrying in a bucket of coals or a branch of candles, would find the two of them lying on the rug in front of the flames, Polly propped against William, their eyes dreamy, their faces flushed red with the fire's heat. But sometimes, William did not come back for several days. On those occasions, when his anger took longer to cool, he went to stay with the Wordsworths, who understood the needs of poets, or the Coleridges, a household with similar problems to his own and hence full of sympathy for his predicament. This was clearly one of those times when William was so troubled that he could not bear to admit his responsibilities or to stay too close to his fretting wife.

—What's a man to do? he was shouting upstairs: I can't go on living like this. I can't write.

Polly's lighter tones answered him, soothing, calming. He could be the baby and she would rock him. She accepted William completely. She bowed down to his talent and worshipped it. But then she didn't have to give birth to his babies year in and year out. That helped her stay devoted, Daisy thought. She got the best of William because she was his friend as well as his sister and could sit up late and talk to him. Although Fanny was occasionally jealous that William shared less of his inner life with her than with Polly, she could hardly complain, because if he was downstairs late at night discussing his latest poem with Polly then he was not upstairs in Fanny's bed making her pregnant. That was how Daisy saw it, anyway. She understood, too, that Fanny was frightened at the thought of giving birth again. In seventeen years of marriage she had borne eight children, four of whom had not lived, and had had two miscarriages. She was bound to be worrying that her luck was running out and that this time she might die.

So Daisy said to her employer now, coaxing her: well, then,

he'll be in a much better temper when he comes back, won't he. Give him time to get over the idea of a new addition to the family and he'll cheer up, you'll see.

Fanny dried her eyes and blew her nose.

—Oh, it's not just the new baby coming that makes him cross. It's all the other upsetting things that have been happening lately. First of all that American business, and now this letter from France.

She hesitated, clearly deciding whether or not to risk taking Daisy further into her confidence. Daisy was affronted, but did not show it. She put on her dim expression, so that Fanny would be tempted to despise her stupidity and reveal more.

—Don't you remember? Fanny said: poor Mr Saygood had that troubling letter from America a month ago. And now he's heard that an old friend of his in France has just died, and there's worse still.

She sighed, and halted her revelations. Daisy got up and dumped Freddy into her arms.

—Please take him, ma'am, I've got the dinner to dish up.

—I do sometimes wonder, Fanny said: why we came up here at all. We're dogged by trouble.

—We came, Daisy said: because Mr Saygood wanted to be close to his poet friends.

She gave the pot of beans a stir. And I came, she thought: to escape from missing Billy so much. And yet I couldn't leave him behind. He turns up in my dreams nearly every night.

Fanny was smiling now, her little finger in Freddy's mouth, her face relaxed.

—I remember the plans we had. We were all going to join forces and live together in a revolutionary commune of total equality. The men were going to share all the cooking and housework and looking after the babies. William drew up a plan, showing the allocation of tasks. I've still got it somewhere. Polly and I were allowed, under the system, three hours every day for our own writing. The idea was that we would all be poets and all be parents.

They heard William rush down the stairs. He put his head round the door and called a brief goodbye. He had been crying. The traces of tears still blotched his cheeks. He snatched a cold pasty and an apple from the larder and disappeared. They heard him shouting to Polly. Then his boots clumped down the path, the gate squeaked open and shut, and he was gone.

Daisy got the dinner on to the table and called the children. Afterwards, Fanny went upstairs to have a nap. The children went back outside to play. Polly took the baby's cot to the furthest end of the garden, so that if he cried no one would hear him. Then she put on her shawl and stomped off for a solitary walk. Daisy washed up and swept the kitchen floor.

Later on she and Polly organised the children into playing horses round the orchard, going over jumps. It tired them out so much they went off to bed without making too much trouble. After supper, Daisy joined the other two women in the parlour, rather than sitting by herself in the kitchen. It saved on candles and coals. While Fanny and Polly read, seated at the little table drawn near the fire so that they could share a candlestick and catch as much warmth as possible, Daisy tackled the mending.

There was a quality of silence between the other two that was not peaceful. Something sharp in it, that could scratch. Like a cat hiding under the table then clawing your ankle when you went by. Daisy licked her thread and poked it through the needle's eye. Not surprising if occasionally the two women wanted to quarrel. They both loved the same man and had to share him. That was all they had in common. They were sisters by marriage but without him, the glue of their lives, they came unstuck, adrift. Their politeness to each other was almost unpleasant. Perhaps William's way was better, more honest, shouting then running off. But Fanny felt she couldn't do that. She had the children to think of. Perhaps she ought to take turns with William, running away for short periods. It might do her good.

—If you're too tired to sew, Daisy, Fanny said: I suggest you go to bed.

She left them to it. Lying on her little truckle bed in the tiny room behind the kitchen, she heard the high darting and stabbing of their voices, like gulls.

Next day dawned cloudless and hot. Fanny herded the children into the parlour and set them to their lessons. Polly helped Daisy sort clothes for the wash. While the weather stayed so fine, it was worth getting on with as much of it as possible. Woollen clothes, in particular, which took so long to dry at any other time of year, could be spread in the sunshine on the hedges bordering the orchard. Coats, blankets, shawls, bodices, trousers, they could do the lot. Daisy ran upstairs, opened the clothes chests in the three bedrooms, brought down one armful after another, tossed them in heaps, according to colour, blue or grey or brown, on the kitchen table.

She lit the fire under the big copper in the back kitchen. While she waited for the water to heat up, she checked the piles of clothes for loose buttons, holes that needed mending. She went through the pockets, removing ancient conkers on strings, handkerchiefs, pennies, a letter, pebbles and shells.

The letter was folded up in the pocket of the trousers William had had on yesterday morning. He must have slipped it in there then forgotten about it. Daisy opened it and flattened it out on the table-top. She couldn't understand a single word of it. The flowing black words kept their secret. Just the signature at the end jumped out at her. A woman's name. Caroline.

She heard Polly clatter down the stairs into the passage just outside. Hastily she threw the letter on to the table with all the other clutter and ran into the back kitchen to be discovered as far away as possible from any suspicion of prying.

Later on, when the afternoon was far advanced, they staggered out with a heavy basket of steaming wet woollens between them. They began to drape them over the hedges.

—We'll have to leave them out all night, they're so wet, Polly said: there's nowhere we can possibly hang them in the house. I just hope they don't get too soaked with dew, or that it doesn't start raining again.

—Oh, it won't rain, Daisy began replying.

She stopped, because she heard a faint voice calling. A cry like a cat. She looked around.

—It must be that beggar come back, she declared: I'll just run out and see what he's up to. We don't want someone loitering about to steal all the clothes as soon as our backs are turned.

The beggar boy collapsed when Daisy shouted at him. He sat down abruptly on the hummock of grass by the gate as though his knees had given way like a puppet's strings being cut. In his distress his voice got higher.

—Please let me in. I must see my father, Mr Saygood.

Polly and Fanny came up, to help Daisy deal with the mischief-maker. Fanny pushed past Polly and looked closely into the boy's face. She gasped as he repeated his pleading words.

—This is some wicked story he's made up in order to get money out of us, she declared: we must get rid of him at once. Daisy, run and fetch help.

The boy had now completely broken down. He had his face in his hands and he was sobbing. Through his tears he was uttering more broken phrases. Annette. The letters.

Fanny and Polly exclaimed loudly. Daisy, moved by curiosity as much as by compassion, raised her hands to hush them. She leaned over the newcomer and spoke gently.

—What is your name, boy? Tell us your name.

—I'm not a boy, I'm a girl, whispered their visitor: and my name is Caroline.

2

—Put her in my room, Daisy panted: behind the kitchen.

The girl was a dead weight in her arms.

—Come on, she cried: d'you want her to die here? She's been touched by the sun, I shouldn't wonder, poor thing.

—Touched in the head, more likely, Polly grumbled.

But she came forward and helped, gripping one side of the stranger's cloak while Fanny unwillingly took hold of the other. Using the cloak as a stretcher, one on each side, they assisted Daisy, who had her hands under the young woman's arms, to get her through the house and so into Daisy's bed. They tipped her into this like a sack of potatoes and she spilled down and was still.

Polly and Fanny went out into the kitchen, leaving Daisy to it. She stripped the clothes off the unconscious girl and put a clean shift on her. Under her clothes she wore a wide, stiff linen belt padded with lumpy pockets. Daisy unbuckled and removed this, and wrapped it up inside the stranger's jacket, deciding to take it away with her next door for a better look. Before going, she pulled up the bedclothes and tucked them loosely around their visitor's shoulders. Her eyes were shut and she was babbling in a low voice, a stream of nonsense words. Daisy couldn't make head or tail of it.

—I'm afraid her wits are gone, she said to Polly.

They were standing together at the kitchen table, turning over the young woman's clothes. They were of good quality, carefully mended and darned. Polly touched the jacket and breeches with her fingertips, for they were very dirty, and had clearly not been washed for some time. Their wearer had clearly travelled nonstop with no change of apparel. Her shoes were caked in mud. Her linen was sweat-stained.

—What's this? Polly said, poking the linen belt.

—I think it's her private possessions, ma'am, Daisy began: her money and such.

Polly was already unfolding it. Her thin fingers prodded the stiff material, then found the looser stitching along the tops of the little pockets. She ripped these open and drew out their contents. A silver thimble. Some shining gold coins. Earrings and a bracelet. A medallion. A tiny framed portrait.

—What's *this*, Polly whispered.

She didn't touch it. Just looked. The miniature, framed in twists of tarnished gilt, winked up at her like an eye. It showed a young man, pink-cheeked and tenderly smiling. His hair was brushed back. His aquiline nose jutted. His eyes were deepset under thin black brows. There was no mistaking the likeness.

—It's William, Polly said: it's definitely William.

Her knuckles beat a faint tattoo on the wooden table-top. Rat-a-tat-tat. A drum warning. Polly was going out to battle.

First of all she held her council of war with Fanny. Both of them visited the stranger, who was still delirious, alternately moaning and babbling. When they bent over her and shook her, she started away from them, her voice going up towards a scream. It took all their strength to keep her from jumping out of bed. After they had gone, Daisy calmed the young woman down, holding her hand and speaking, in a low voice, cosseting words such as she used to the children when they woke up from nightmares. Slowly the stranger relaxed again. She turned over and faced the wall and went back to her chattering.

Fanny and Polly were determined to get rid of the girl

before William came back. When Daisy unlatched the parlour door and slipped through with their hot milk on a tray, she heard the high, excited note in Fanny's voice even before she deciphered her words.

—I mustn't be upset. Not in my condition. William would never forgive himself if I were made ill. How dare this person just turn up and cause such a commotion?

—We'll fetch the doctor to her tomorrow, Polly responded: he'll know exactly what to do. He's dealt with mad people before, I'll be bound.

Daisy placed her tray on the table by the window. She came forward and knelt in front of the fire, to build it up better. She kept her head down so that they wouldn't see her listening but would go on thinking she was a footstool or suchlike.

—And William must have peace and quiet for his writing when he returns, Fanny said: we've had so many visitors already this summer, he's been nearly driven to distraction, poor dear man.

Daisy retreated, wiping her dirty hands, black with coal dust, on her apron. She backed away slowly, towards the door. Neither of them noticed her as she crept out. She felt that she ought to help the stranger and stand up for her, but she did not know what to do. She shelved matters by making herself a bed of cushions in front of the kitchen fire and falling asleep.

3

The girl sat up. She was wild-eyed, incoherent. She wouldn't let Daisy near her to wash her face with the proffered flannel soaked in soapy water. She would not consent to her hair being brushed.

—Don't be a silly thing, Daisy scolded her: can't you see you'll do much better with the doctor if he sees you looking clean and in your right mind like a Christian?

The girl stared at her. Daisy made a decision. It wasn't only concern for the visitor's welfare. Curiosity also played its part. She enunciated slowly and clearly.

—Your father would want you to look nice. Mr William Saygood, your father. He would want you to look decent, now, wouldn't he?

The girl sat up in bed. She spoke her first coherent words since collapsing the day before. Her English sounded odd, but Daisy could understand what she said.

—My father is Mr William Saygood. He lives here, in this house. I am his daughter Caroline. His house is called La Colombe.

It was like a lesson she had learned off by heart. She looked hopefully at Daisy, a pupil seeking approval.

From behind them came a voice like a stern teacher's, slapping down a correction.

—Mr William Saygood is not your father. You are not his daughter. It's all a tale of nonsense.

Polly's voice. Polly stood in the doorway, her face pinched and white, her hands shaking.

—You're mad, she said: quite mad and wicked, even to imagine such a thing.

The girl gave a loud cry. She sprang out of bed, looking so fierce she took the other two by surprise. She was like a hunted creature making its dash for freedom. Before they had collected their wits to step forwards and stop her she had run past them out of the door. When they rushed after her, she cried out loud again, opened the back door from the main kitchen, and vanished outside into the garden.

At this moment the doctor's chaise drew up outside. Now there ensued a certain fuss and hullabaloo. Polly flew to the parlour to command the children, on pain of slaps and no dinner, to stay inside until let out. Fanny came down the stairs, demanding in her high querulous voice what all the noise was about? Daisy opened the front door to the doctor and brought him into the passageway. Then she, Fanny and Polly all began speaking at once, explaining what had happened.

He shooed them in front of him out of the house, by the back door. There the four of them stopped and sent their eyes swerving about, looking for the girl.

They had not far to seek. She stood at the far end of the path, by the orchard gate. At the sound of their footsteps on the gravel she turned and faced them. Her short hair sprang out wildly round her face. Her shift was pulled awry, half hanging off one shoulder. Her feet were bare. She clasped her hands together in a gesture of supplication. She gazed at the doctor.

—Father, she faltered: I am Caroline. I am the daughter of William Saygood.

—You see what I mean? Fanny hissed: the poor thing is completely deluded. Her mind is quite gone.

Caroline opened her arms and smiled like a little girl of ten. The contrast between her beaming childlike face and torn, revealing clothes was grotesque. It made them wriggle with embarrassment. Her arms and legs were bare under the skimpy shift and her breasts showed. Her face gleamed with happiness. She advanced towards the doctor, as though to embrace him.

—Papa, she said: my dear Papa.

This is no place for her, Daisy thought in a rush of pain, here outside, oh let me take her back indoors and put her to bed again, poor thing, she'll be better after a long rest, she's worn out from travelling, that's all, anyone can see that, she's not mad.

Polly put her hand on the doctor's arm.

—Be careful. She looks meek as a kitten but she's very strong. She'll spring at you, given half a chance. You should have seen how she fought us earlier on this morning, when we were trying to attend to her in her bed. She's got the strength of ten men.

Caroline halted. She lowered her arms and wrapped them around herself, shivering in the breeze. Now she looked merely bewildered.

—Papa? she said: Papa?

—It's all right, Mrs Saygood, the doctor returned to Fanny: I've brought help. Now please get back to the house, ladies, and leave this to me.

He whistled, and two men came out of the kitchen. Daisy supposed they must have come with the doctor in his carriage. They were big, burly men, with impassive faces. They crept up on Caroline as though she were a lion and they the brave hunters armed with nets and spears. It was a sort of net they threw over her at a sign from the doctor, a canvas net with ties and straps. In a trice she was caught and bound and screaming. A canvas gag over her mouth soon stopped her cries. While the three women of the household cowered against the wall, too ashamed to watch, the two hunters picked up their prey by the bound elbows, dragged her down the path, and pushed her inside the waiting carriage. The doctor touched his hat to Fanny and Polly and followed them. In a moment more, the carriage was off, clattering away down the village street and rapidly out of sight behind the houses.

Fanny had to be looked after. She was in such a state of near-hysteria that there was no time for discussion or speculation, certainly no time for regrets. They supported her into the parlour and chafed her wrists and mopped her brow with a cloth soaked in cologne. The children, used to their mother's fainting fits, crowded through the door and off to games outside. Daisy opened the window to let in some fresh air, then stood next to Fanny and fanned her with her apron.

—Oh my poor darling children, Fanny exclaimed in a faint voice: to be in the same house as a lunatic. Thanks be to God that they escaped unscathed.

She burst into loud tears.

—Now come on, Polly said: the danger's over, they've taken her away and we're well rid of her and she'll never be able to come back here and make trouble again.

—What have I done to deserve it? Fanny wept: to be threatened in my own home by a madwoman?

Daisy walked over to the door.

—It's all right, Polly said: she'll be safely locked up in the asylum at York and that's the last you'll ever hear of her. Don't talk about her any more. Hush.

Fanny could not stop trembling.

—When I think of it, she whispered: we could all have been murdered in our beds.

All these speeches were lies, Daisy knew. Fanny would swear to William, if she had to, that she had been in terrible fear. And Daisy would be forced to be a witness. Yes, sir, Mrs Saygood *did* say she was certain the young woman was mad.

Fanny turned her head to speak to the retreating Daisy.

—It's all your fault. You made us take her in. We should never have let her across the threshold.

She was in for a long fit of nerves and crying, Daisy saw. So she went quietly out and into the kitchen. Everything she looked at had Caroline's face etched into it, Caroline's burning eyes. What else could I have done? she said to Caroline: I didn't know the doctor was going to have you put away. I should have done something, but what? She was so upset that before night-fall she had smacked each and every child. Her fingers itched to slap Fanny and Polly too. The substitute came in a bottle of medicine which stroked them rather than bludgeoned them into docility. Blessed opium which healed and soothed, Daisy thought. Opium, the servant's friend, which sent ladies to sleep and stopped their fretting and fussing.

4

Everybody except Daisy was in bed, candles extinguished and curtains pulled. Her own nightlight was a tallow dip. She carried it in one hand as she crept up the stairs. Her boots she left behind in the kitchen so that she would make less noise. Smothering the sound of her breathing on her sleeve she stood on the tiny landing, listening to the snores coming from the three rooms around it. The fourth room, built out at the back over the kitchen, was William's library. He retreated up here to write when visitors dropped in and the parlour was in use. Daisy lifted the latch gently and slipped inside.

She knew only roughly what she was hunting for. Two letters had arrived and caused trouble, hadn't they? One of them, the one sent by the unfortunate French girl Caroline, had been left by William in his trouser pocket and picked out by Daisy when she sorted the wash. After Caroline had been taken away, Fanny had rolled up all her things and carried them off upstairs, presumably to hide them. The letter she had dropped on to the parlour fire. What a pity, she would say to William, if he asked for the letter, that he had left it in his trouser pocket. It had been rendered soggy and illegible by the wash and so Fanny had had to throw it away. How unfortunate. Daisy could just hear her cooing out the words and daring William to disprove them.

Fanny did not mind telling lies when she had to. When she felt she had to protect her own interests. She had represented the French girl to the doctor as deluded, wicked and mad, a penniless vagrant with no friends or family or home. But she had not dared to get rid of the girl's possessions. The jewellery and the miniature. Perhaps she was simply biding her time, while she worked out the next stage of her plan. In a month or two, who knew? Fanny might easily decide to destroy Caroline's belongings, or sell them in secret. She might easily manage to keep William in total ignorance of the entire episode.

Daisy was looking for the second letter in the mystery, the one from America. It was quite easy to find, because William was so neat. All his papers were carefully organised. Poetry lay on the table by the window, a slippage of loose sheets covered by William's curly black scrawl, decorated with ink blots where he had impatiently shaken the pen, crossings-out where the nib scratched through one word after another. A stack of poems in Polly's flowing writing sat to one side. These were the corrected versions, dictated in the parlour after supper. The fair copies, that William sent off to his publishers in London. Daisy saw that there were no other sorts of document here, so she turned her attention to his little writing-desk. Under the flapped-back lid was a space divided into compartments, each one stuffed with rolls of papers. Bills, receipts, several bundles of letters. The letter from Paul Gilbert in Kentucky was on its own. She recognised the name immediately. She had heard him mentioned often enough, one of the friends of William's youth, a bit of a rover, an adventurer. The confident flourishing signature leaped up at her from the page. She lifted her candle to see better, making sure that drops of tallow did not fall on the paper she held in her other hand, and peered at what the French gentleman had to say. Luckily he had written in English. She drew in her breath as she read, in a hiss of surprise.

Something had to be done about all of this, Daisy decided.

All those years ago, Fanny had hurt her very badly, sending Billy away. Now she had hurt Caroline, sending her away too. At long last, Daisy saw a chance of getting revenge for the one injury, and limiting the other. She was clear now about whom to ask to help. She turned and rummaged again in William's writing-desk, until she found the address she wanted. Then she crept back downstairs.

William returned two days later. The woollens wash was done, the ironing completed and the clothes folded and put away. A pleasant smell of soap hung about the house so that it seemed far cleaner than it really was. He came back at dusk, just as Daisy was serving the children their supper of bread and milk in the kitchen. Commanding them not to stir, because their frisking welcome disturbed him if he was tired and made him cross, she went to the front door and opened it. He walked past her into the parlour. She looked past him, to see what he saw. There sat his wife and sister in harmonious silence, one knitting and the other darning. A small fire glowed in the grate. Both of them looked up and smiled at him in welcome. Tenderness and gladness shone from their faces. Their white caps framed their faces like the wings of doves, spotless and pure. He walked over and grasped each one in turn by the hand, kissing them and returning their fond smiles.

PART NINE

St Paul's Churchyard

1

The bell downstairs tinkled again.

—I'm coming, Jemima called: I'm coming.

She herself had bought the bell, as a present for Mr Jackson, years ago. She had donated it to him because she felt he needed it. Sometimes he liked to sit in his workroom behind the shop, mending bindings or scanning proofs, so that he was invisible to anyone who came in. Some of these visitors were on urgent business and stormed at being kept waiting. Now, they could seize the little brass bell sitting on top of the counter and summon Mr Jackson with its clanging tongue. One of Jemima's habits was to help him out when necessary, in gratitude for her low rent. She would stand at the desk downstairs, checking the accounts, writing in the spiky but legible hand she had learned at Miss Wollstonecraft's school in Newington Green over twenty years before. She helped pack up parcels of books. She read and corrected proofs. She sprinted up and down stairs carrying messages and trays of food. She liked all these jobs. They helped her to feel connected to the outside world. So she always kept an ear cocked for the bell, in case Mr Jackson had gone into the printing workshop and could not hear it, or indeed was summoning her to join him and a favoured visitor over a glass of wine or a cup of tea. In this way, she made many valuable acquaintances, whose brains she picked shamelessly for her novels.

Mr Jackson's intimates visited in the evenings, when the shop was shut up and the fire lit upstairs in his parlour on the first floor. People often stayed to supper, and she sometimes made one of the party. It depended on her whim. When poets and writers came to eat, she contrived to take her place in the group, but when the gathering was philosophers only, she generally stayed away. Not so much because she disliked philosophy but because Godwin would come, and his austere face brought back such painful memories of Mary Wollstonecraft, dead three days after giving birth to Godwin's daughter, that Jemima could not always bear it. Miss Wollstonecraft had stayed on in Paris throughout the Terror; she had had her own love affair and had borne a child as a result of it. She had returned to London, to work, and to care for her little daughter, and eventually to take up with Godwin, though she would not live with him. She and Jemima had met again, and gathered up the old threads of conversation, as seasoned radicals who had seen one revolution, in France, and hoped to see another, in England. Inspired by Miss Wollstonecraft, determined to follow her example, Jemima had wanted to do great things. But with the older woman clawed down by death in childbed, her ambitions had shrunk. She wrote her novels and her articles and listened to the political conversations in Mr Jackson's parlour. She was a radical who had learned to keep her head down, like so many of the people she knew.

Steadying the taper she had lit from her dying fire, she tapped down the bare wooden stairs. On the landing below, she found the bell placed at the top of the next flight, and a letter lying next to it. Mr Jackson's parlour door was just closing. His voice grunted through the crack.

—Sorry, Miss Boote. This came for you earlier and I took it in. Forgot to give it to you. Goodnight.

—Thank you, called Jemima to the closed door.

She picked up the letter and bore it back upstairs. Inside her rooms again, she went over to the window-seat. She kept the shutters open until late at night, so that she could look out on the glimmering dome of St Paul's. She hung the candlestick from a hook in the side of the window, sat down, and opened her letter. She looked at the signature first. Daisy Dollcey. Jemima blinked. This was strange. Very occasionally she heard from William or Fanny, but never from their maid. There must be something wrong. She spread the letter flat on her knee, bent over it, and began intently to read.

Letters were rare in Jemima's life. Her brother Ned lived not far away from her, in the house he had inherited from his god-father in Clerkenwell, but he was a busy lawyer, with too much well-paid business on his hands to waste time visiting his sister, let alone writing to her. While she herself, being far too proud and haughty, went to see him rarely and hardly ever wrote to him. It was her duty as the unmarried one, with time on her hands, to keep up a dutiful correspondence, but she did not. She wrote twice a year, at Christmas and Easter, and that was that. As for her brother and sisters in Ireland, she did not even know their address. They were long lost to her and she to them.

To receive a letter was to receive a treat. Usually, she tried to read slowly, to make the pleasure last. But the surprise of hearing from Daisy was so great, her desire to understand the reasons for it so strong, that she consumed the letter eagerly, her eyes racing along the lines of writing and her mouth dropping open with shock as she read what Daisy had to say.

She leaned forwards, clutching herself. The news was like a fist hitting her stomach.

They took her away, Daisy wrote, tied up in canvas, without her clothes, I cannot get her out poor thing but you must ma'am you can do it.

2

All the way up to York in the plodding coach, Jemima was tormented by the thought of Annette's daughter locked up among hostile strangers, lonely and frightened, perhaps unable to speak a word of English. Her incarceration must be Fanny's doing, she thought. Jealous of Annette, that William had once loved her so much he had had a child by her, she wouldn't have wanted Annette's daughter in her house, not for one minute. But where had William been while it was all happening? Surely it had not been done with his consent. Jemima had written to him before setting off, to tell him where she was going, and why, and she hoped desperately he would not allow himself to be prevented from coming to her assistance. She had no idea how she was going to get Caroline out of the asylum. She was not related to her in any way. She had no proof that she had known her mother. But why had Caroline turned up in England at all? How on earth had she managed the journey, all on her own? The questions whirled about Jemima's brain as they plunged north through scouring winds and sheeting wet.

In York she hired a gig at the inn where she was set down in the middle of the city, and had herself driven to the asylum, newly built, outside the ramparts, on the outskirts of town. On arrival she paid off half her fare and asked the driver to wait for her. There was another carriage standing under the dripping trees near the lodge gate. The man holding the horses shouted a rough greeting to her, and pointed out which way to go.

The pointed archway framing the gate let her in through the high wall. The battlemented top made it seem like a medieval castle. At the end of a drive which led under massed trees, through some kind of gloomy garden, the asylum reared before her, a great blank façade pierced with small windows in mock-perpendicular style. Jemima shuddered. Then she stepped forward, to what appeared to be the front door, and tugged at the bell.

3

The curly-haired maidservant who opened the door showed Jemima across a cold, dark hall to an anteroom, telling her to wait while she went to see if the Superintendent was free.

—He's been busy all morning with a visitor, she remarked: and now he's still having his dinner, I dare say.

—Please tell him it's urgent, Jemima said: I've come a long way. It's really important. There's been a terrible mistake.

—He only sees visitors with an appointment, the maid returned: you'll have to wait.

She shut the door of the anteroom. Her footsteps clacked away. Jemima, stumbling forwards into the dimness, did not at first see the tall figure who rose to greet her. Then she caught her breath. He was thinner than formerly, with hair beginning to recede from his temples, but his smile was just the same.

—William. You've come, Jemima said: thank goodness.

—I had to, he said: this whole business is my fault. If I'd been at home, it couldn't have happened. Poor Fanny, she was so frightened by Caroline falling ill. I should have been there.

He looked anxious and careworn. His face was pale, and he kept rubbing his hand against the side of his nose as he talked. He was bound to defend Fanny, Jemima thought. He had to live with her, after all.

—Never mind that, she said: where's Caroline? Will they let

me see her? I'm going to take her back to London with me. Then we'll decide what to do. How is she? Have you seen her? Where are they keeping her, in this awful place?

—She's all right, William said: she's upstairs, you can't see her for a little while, the doctor's with her, they're getting her ready to leave. They've got to get her dressed and so on. I've seen the Superintendent already and explained the circumstances. I've been able to prove Caroline's identity, thanks to the letters and papers I brought with me. We'll be able to leave here with her very soon. Apparently she is quite weak still, but rapidly regaining her strength. She'll be all right.

He sounded very tired. He sounded guilty. Jemima thought that his eyes were saying: please don't be too angry.

—It's very good of you to say you'll take her in, William added.

—Where else could she go? Jemima asked: we both know there is no possible chance of her living with you.

She paced about the dreary little room.

—If we've got to wait, she said: why don't we wait outside? I'd like to get some air. I don't care if it's raining. I hate this place.

William hesitated. He seemed very tense. Then he nodded.

—Yes. Let's do that.

The drizzle had ceased. They walked up and down for a few moments on the damp gravel outside the front door, and then Jemima, wanting to get further away from the brooding house, wandered towards the side of the lawn, and the long walk of lime trees which led away from it.

Despite the season, the air was chilly. Though it was only late afternoon the sun seemed already waning. Some of the trees were turning yellow and dropping the odd withered leaf upon the grass. Jemima shivered, suddenly depressed. It was only August, yet autumn seemed to be beginning. She drew her cloak around herself and bent her head against the breeze which tugged her hair out from under her hat and blew it into her eyes.

At her side William paced in thoughtful silence. When they

reached the end of the walk he paused and Jemima paused with him. A stone balustrade rose up here, marking the end of the path, and with one accord they turned and leaned their elbows on it, looking at the stream which flowed past on the other side.

—I don't know how to tell you this, William said at last: but I must tell you. It is not right that you should be kept in ignorance.

Jemima was idly watching a thrush hop along the ground.

—Why? she said: what is it?

Some little scruple about Fanny's presumed part in all this sad business, she supposed. She was in no way prepared for his next words.

—Jemima, William began: has it not occurred to you that this French girl, although we may assume her to be certainly not mad, may still be in great confusion about her identity?

Jemima turned to look at him in surprise.

—No, she said: how could it? I don't know anything about what's been going on. Daisy's letter was very brief. All it said was that Caroline had been incarcerated here. I've been hoping you could explain.

William returned her gaze. He looked embarrassed, almost ashamed, but he ploughed on determinedly.

—From what Fanny told me, I gather she and Polly told this girl she wasn't my daughter. That was what upset her so much. They weren't lying, Jemima. My daughter by Annette died when she was only a couple of weeks old. We know, Fanny and Polly and I, that that unfortunate young woman in there is not my daughter, as she is not the daughter of Annette Villon either.

—Then who is she? Jemima gasped.

William's voice seemed to have faded, as though he were at the end of a tunnel. His face was distant, as if a mist had crossed it. His words rattled into her listening silence like stones flung down a well.

—She's your daughter, Jemima. She is Paul Gilbert's daughter and yours.

—No. She can't be.

Jemima's voice was so hoarse she didn't recognise it as her own at all. Someone else gripped her hands together so tightly the kid gloves split. Someone else shot a wave of coldness through her, which spoke. How cruel of him to remind her of that tragedy, all those years ago. It was not her thinking that. She was numb. She could feel nothing. It was too cold. The coldness opened her mouth and made her talk.

—It's impossible, she said: my little daughter is dead. You know that. She died at Le Havre, when I went there to search for Paul, just after she was born.

—Let's sit down, William said.

Gently he prised her hands apart with his own. Then he tucked her hand under his arm and led her back down the way they had come, to a bench set in just under the trees. Its feet were covered in drifts of leaves. Something was all wrong, the leaves blowing down too early and poor Caroline locked up and little Maria dead and William teasing her. They sat down on the wooden bench, close together. William took her hand and held it tightly.

—Think back, he said: to when your child was born. There were you and Annette, both in the same house. You both gave birth on the same day, remember?

—Of course I remember, Jemima snapped: how could I possibly forget? What are you trying to say? Go on. Spit it out.

William sighed. He kicked a leaf with his foot.

—I had a letter from Paul about a month ago, he said: from America, telling me what he'd done. God knows why he wrote. To mock me? To humiliate me? To apologise? All of those, perhaps. His reasons for writing were not clear. He didn't spell them out. He chose to write in English, and perhaps that allowed him to keep his letter brief.

—But what did he say? Jemima interrupted.

She wasn't at all sure she would be able to take it in. The world was beginning to revolve slowly around her, as if the bench were spinning, a blur of golden-green-grey as the leaves blew about. She felt faint and sick.

William was enunciating slowly and carefully.

—Paul exchanged the babies, he said: yours and Annette's. He got the servant girl, what was her name, Louise, to swap them in their cradles, on the day he arrived, in the evening of the day they were born. He did it as a sort of joke, I think.

—But why? Jemima whispered.

William let go of her hand. He shifted about on the seat. When he spoke, his voice sounded uncomfortable. Well, how else could it sound? Jemima thought. She tried to listen carefully to what he was saying, but she had the oddest impression that the wind was trying to take his words and hurl them away as though they were dead leaves. Or a dead baby that she had thought for eighteen years was hers.

—You know what Paul was like, he said: you of all people. He had very passionate convictions. He and I argued a lot about the perfectibility of man, how much a revolution could change human beings, whether human nature could actually be reformed by politics. Well, so he decided to put it to the test. He decided to perform an experiment. Fair exchange was no robbery. That was how he put it, in his letter.

William sounded tired. All this explaining he had to do. Jemima was tired too. She wanted to lie on the ground and let the wind cover her with leaves, stuff them into her mouth and ears so that she could not cry and could not hear any more about what the man she had loved had done.

—Paul thought, William went on: that the two babies would receive such different upbringings, for example as regards religion, that after eighteen years or so they could be compared, to see what function their blood had played. Whether his baby would be like him, despite having been brought up Catholic and Royalist. He wanted to know whether it would turn out a fiery little Republican notwithstanding.

Jemima got to her feet. She had to stand up, to fend off William's ridiculous and impossible words.

—Let's walk a little. It's too cold to stay sitting down for long. My brain feels thick with ice.

They walked slowly back towards the blank stone façade of the house.

—I don't believe you, Jemima said: no, not about Paul exchanging the babies, he was certainly capable of that. His morality was not the same as mine, or Annette's, that's certain.

She paused, so that William, holding her elbow, had to pause too. She looked at him directly, forcing him to look back.

—There's another reason, isn't there, for what he did? I don't believe he did it just out of scientific curiosity, or as a horrible joke. He was trying to hurt us, wasn't he? It was his way of saying he didn't want to be a father and didn't care about his child.

The tears were coursing down her face. While she waited for William's reply she blotted her eyes on her sleeves. She had lost her handkerchief somewhere. She wanted to blow her nose but she couldn't.

—I don't suppose he fully realised at the time what he was doing, William said: if you remember, he and I got very drunk, celebrating. His judgement, let alone his conscience, must have been completely clouded over. I don't think he was entirely responsible for what he was doing. And then, later on, when he realised what he'd done, when he was sober again, he didn't know how to put things right without being caught. He was afraid of our finding out.

—And that, I suppose, Jemima said: was another reason why he ran away so soon.

They had reached the massive front door of the asylum. She lifted her hand and pulled the bellpull. She felt very weary. Her mind was in a muddle. Too many conflicting feelings chased round inside. She did not have time to go into them now. She squashed them down under a coldness which she knew concealed great anger. She had a long and tiring journey ahead, with a sick and probably frightened companion to take care of. She had to reserve all her energy for that. Her voice, when she spoke, was formal and cool. Coldness was good. It kept control of a woman who wanted to scream and howl like a lunatic.

—It was good of you to come and explain all of this to me, William. If you hadn't arrived to help me, I doubt whether I'd ever have been able to get Caroline out of here.

She stopped, and gulped. Not Caroline. Maria. She fought to keep her voice steady.

—Let's write to each other, anyway. I'll write to you and tell you how Caroline gets on.

The curly-haired maidservant opened the door and stood waiting for them to enter. William hovered indecisively. Jemima could see that he wanted to run away again. She didn't blame him. She thought she would like to do the same herself. Run away from this cold. Leave this girl behind like a dead baby you bury in the snow.

—I think I'll go now, William said: Caroline's had enough shocks for the moment. I don't think she needs to see me. You explain it all to her. You can speak French better than I, that's certain. Once she's recovered a little, you tell her.

He jerked his head towards the hall.

—There's a little parcel of her things in there that I brought with me. Bits and pieces of jewellery. She left them behind at La Colombe. Don't forget to take them.

—Wait, Jemima said.

She struggled to find the words.

—William, I can't cope with any of this. What you've told me. What shall I do? How will I manage? How do I know I'm doing the right thing, taking her home with me?

William looked at her hopelessly. Tears stood in his eyes.

—I'll write to you very soon, he said: there is a lot more to say that we can't say now. Forgive me for not helping more. I'm sorry, Jemima.

They kissed each other on both cheeks. Then she left him there at the door, and followed the woman upstairs to find her daughter.

4

On the journey back to London Caroline did not speak a word. She slept a lot. It was a retreat into herself, Jemima thought, and she was glad of it, for it protected the girl from the curiosity of their travelling companions. Caroline was docile, alighting from the coach when they stopped at inns for the night, obediently eating her supper then climbing into bed. The only garments she had with her were her linen underclothes, and an old woollen dress and pelisse of Fanny's that William had brought for her. He had explained to Jemima about the male clothes she had arrived in. Luckily, Jemima had had the foresight to bring a nightgown with her, a change of underwear. Comb and hairbrush, she also supplied herself.

In London she put Caroline to bed, uncertain whether she really needed treating like an invalid, yet anxious to make her feel as safe as possible. Bed was her own refuge in times of trouble, the curtains pulled against depression, the covers pulled up over her head, so she imagined it might be Caroline's too. And in any case, a good night's sleep never did anyone any harm. Having seen her visitor close her eyes, she departed softly next door, to eat supper with Mr Jackson. He had ordered in a dish of baked chops and a bottle of wine, and she told him the whole story of her journey while they ate. Later on, when he had gone off to his own rooms on the floor below, she made herself a bed on three chairs, thinking that Caroline might prefer not to have to share hers with a stranger.

In the morning she was up early. She folded back the shutters to let the sun stream in and to see the dome of St Paul's curve huge and white into the sky. She swept the room and watered the plants and fed the cat. She lit a fire in the grate and put water on to boil for coffee. Then she ran downstairs into the street to fetch some hot rolls for breakfast, a can of milk, and a piece of butter.

She found she was walking around the room humming, all her senses alert. The nightmare journey was over and she was home again. These two small rooms with their astonishing view really were home; and her daughter lay asleep next door. She was rather nervous as she covered her wooden writing-table with a white cloth and laid out her entire stock of china: two cups and saucers, two plates, two fluted, oval dishes to hold the butter and the rolls, wrapped in a white cloth, a coffee pot and milk jug. She had no idea how they were going to get on.

A soft tap at the inner door was followed by Caroline's face looking round it.

—Come in, Jemima said, going across the room and taking her by the hand: have you slept well?

She spoke in French, as she had on the journey back from York. Caroline's face lit up. Like a door opening into a room to show you the glow of lamps inside. For the first time, she seemed to understand what was said to her.

—You speak French, she exclaimed: are you, then, French?

—No, Jemima said: but I learned French at school, and then, when I was young, I lived in Paris for a while.

A look of wariness, of uncertainty, crossed Caroline's face. Jemima tugged gently at her hand.

—Come and sit down. We can talk while you eat. You are looking so much stronger today. I'm really pleased to see you so recovered.

—I did sleep very well, Caroline said: I've been asleep for days and days, I think, and now I've woken up.

She's young and healthy, Jemima thought: and she has survived a great deal. There's not too much wrong with her that I can see. But poor thing, there are yet more shocks coming her way. I hope she really is tough enough to cope.

She wheeled the table in between the two chairs that were set one on each side of the cheerfully blazing fire. Caroline sank down and looked around. Jemima saw the room through her eyes: the sunshine streaming in on to the whitish floor and painted panelling, the clump of flowering plants, the worn pink and yellow Turkey rug, the heaps of books and papers. She smelled the hot coffee and rolls, the perfume of the flowers. When she saw Caroline sitting there opposite it was as though a huge smile opened up inside her. Joy flooded her like the sunshine pouring into the room. Everything was very simple. She was sitting having breakfast with her daughter. Her lost daughter had returned and they were together again. It was true. She was not dreaming.

—Oh my Persephone, Jemima said.

She stretched out her hand for Caroline's cup and poured her some coffee.

5

It seemed to Jemima, when she looked back on this time in years to come, that she and Caroline existed inside a bubble of innocence, as though they had both just been born. Eden-like, this place they lived in together, spun out of words and sunlight, the growing easiness between them. Love. It sprang up like a plant and flourished. Love had grown Caroline inside her and now love grew them both.

As well as loving her, she found that she liked her daughter. Her courage, her determination, her independence. The way she stared at things, with her fists clenched at her sides, standing balanced on the balls of her feet, a little pugilist. The way her hair sprang out from her head as though it had too much energy to lie still and flat. The way her strange eyes changed colour, blue or green or greeny-blue according to what she wore. The way she spoke, hesitating and searching for the right words, wanting to make herself clear.

They moved towards each other, step by step. Getting to know one another, discovering each other's histories, was accomplished at the speed and rhythm they worked out together, like a sort of dance, advancing and retreating, bowing and spinning, sometimes smiling and sometimes grave. Caroline had no memory of parts of her adventure. She had only the haziest recollection of her journey north and her arrival at William's house. Those were episodes that for the moment she preferred to leave alone.

They talked to each other while they worked. Jemima had taken up her housekeeper's duties once again, and Caroline followed her about, darting with her from kitchen to shop to store room to print workshop. The charm of this talking, their two lines of words curving around each other like swallows in flight, was that they had two languages to play with. Often they spoke in French, the tongue Jemima loved to speak, feeling reconnected through speech to so many of the important events of her past, to a place where she had suffered and yet also been so happy. Speaking French did more than keep the past alive. It brought it vividly into the present, so that at one and the same time Jemima was the woman of forty with grey threads in her hair and the hopeful girl plunged into the thick of the beginnings of the Revolution and trying to make sense of it all.

Jemima swam in and out of the knowledge that Caroline was her daughter, and Caroline did the same.

—Annette was my mother too, she insisted: she brought me up. My name is Caroline, not Maria.

She could not always grasp what Paul had done. They went over and over this ground together, both of them bewildered and hurt, both full of questions and both angry. They talked of Louise, and her complicity. They sat down together and wrote a letter to Maître Robert, explaining that Caroline was safe, with her English friends, telling him about the trick that Paul had played.

Caroline gradually awoke from her protective numbness. Her grief for Annette began to emerge, as she dared to remember her. She had wept for Annette before, but now she had to begin all over again. She discovered that Annette was not completely lost to her. She was there, intact and undamaged, in her memory, even as she was etched there by lines of absence. Caroline wept for Annette in bursts of tears that came and went like thunderstorms. When the pain was too all-enveloping she talked in English. Expressing herself in a foreign language was so difficult that less emotion spilled through. As she wrestled with grammar and vocabulary, searching haltingly for her words, so she put a shape and form on grief. In French it flowed out like a stream and in English it was the stepping-stones across.

Mr Jackson, in his taciturn, unobtrusive way, made friends with Caroline. He presented her with a pair of gloves, a gilt ribbon, some books. He encouraged her to spend time downstairs in the shop, to leave her mother time for her writing upstairs. He offered Jemima a third attic room, which she gratefully accepted, in which Caroline could sleep. They cleared out the junk it contained, painted the walls blue, and carried up a bed and chair.

Jemima felt they had sailed out of the storm and groped their way to a safe harbour. Here they were waiting for the winds to die down before putting to sea again. Caroline's voyage was incomplete because her father had vanished. She peered into his absence, and wondered.

She began to pronounce words that Jemima had not heard her speak before, in a new language; a third language; the language of father-love. I wonder where my father is. I wonder what he is like. I wonder if he loves me.

—You see, the peculiar thing, Caroline said: is that I have had three fathers so far. Or thought I did. It nearly drove me mad, having to discard the first two of them. So this third one, this newest one, I can't help wanting to meet him. To get to know him. Part of me comes from him but I don't know what. I want to find out.

Jemima marvelled at her determination. First of all she had cast her line from France to England. Now, to hook her fish, she was wading further out, casting from England to America.

—So what do you want to do? she asked.

—I want to go to America to find my father, Caroline said: my mind is quite made up. William can give me the address. You said he's got it. I'll write and say I'm coming, and then I shall sell all the jewellery I brought with me from France, to pay for the boat. And then I'll see what to do next, when I get there.

—You are certainly like Paul in one thing, Jemima told her: and that's your determination to leave me.

She was half laughing, half crying.

—I knew this must happen, she said: but I wasn't expecting it quite so soon. I'm only just getting to know you. But I do see that you must go, if you really want to. I know that you will, you're so stubborn.

Caroline kissed her.

—That's the part of me that takes after you.

6

—Promise me that you're not going away for ever, Jemima said: promise me that you'll come back.

She held Caroline so tightly that her daughter could not move. Caroline's face, wet with tears, was against hers. Their tears slid between their cheeks and mixed.

Caroline's voice was muffled.

—I promise.

Jemima let go of her. Caroline's luggage was already packed into the boot of the mail coach. All she had to do was spring in. Then the steps were folded up after her and she was waving to her mother as the driver twirled his whip over the horses' heads, the horn was blown, and they set off away from Charing Cross, heading north. Jemima turned, and went east, towards Fleet Street, and St Paul's.

She had promised Caroline not to mope, and she tried not to. It was always harder, she thought, for the one who stayed at home, who did not depart on an adventure. So she decided to allow herself small adventures. She went out for long walks, roaming through all the parts of London she did not know well. She had her hair cut in a fashionable and becoming style. She had two new dresses made, one in black muslin with white spots, and the other in blue, with white stripes. She finished her novel ahead of time, and threw a supper-party to celebrate, at which everybody got tipsy and told bawdy stories and sang.

Mr Jackson noticed her restlessness. He invited her out to the theatre, to see a new production of *The Tempest*. Jemima, unable not to think of Caroline voyaging off to her brave new world, wept discreetly into her handkerchief. She enjoyed the expedition, and the stroll round Covent Garden afterwards, and the late supper in Soho. Over a bottle of wine they talked. Mr Jackson forgot to be taciturn, and told funny stories about all the writers who had been coming to his shop over the past twenty years, their foibles and furies. They compared notes on Mary Wollstonecraft. Jemima told him about her time in France, which she had never done before. They agreed to go together to the theatre again, and to the opera.

This new cheerfulness got Jemima through the knowledge that her daughter had sailed away. Caroline's plan had been to travel up to the Lakes, to Greydale, and to visit William briefly at La Colombe. While she had no wish to see Fanny and Polly ever again, she wanted to meet properly the man Annette had loved so much. Then she would embark for America from Liverpool. The letter arrived from William in due course, confirming that the visit had gone well, and that he had seen Caroline safely on to her ship and into the company of the family of emigrants who had promised to keep an eye out for her during the voyage. Caroline had scrawled a note under William's signature, sending love and saying *au revoir*.

Jemima walked away from St Paul's Churchyard, after receiving this letter, and down Godliman Street towards the river, hurrying between the warehouses in Stew Lane and emerging on to the jetty at the end. She leaned her elbows on the wooden balustrade and gazed at the brown silky waters, the tide streaming fast. Gulls tumbled overhead, crying, swooping for food. Boats plied past, upstream and down. The calls of watermen mingled with the shouts of men unloading cargoes on the quays. The wind grabbed her hat and cloak, shaking them. She put up both hands to her hat brim, holding it tightly.

She gazed at the wind-whipped clouds, the river which pushed along like a strong brown animal flexing brown muscles under a brown satin skin. She thought she could taste salt on her lips, from the distant and invisible sea.

EPILOGUE

Saintange-sur-Seine

The room had become so dim that Louise could hardly make out the figure of the priest slumped in his chair opposite. The afternoon light was waning under the approach of rain. The small windows showed the clouds covering the sky with a sheet of grey. The fire had died down, and Louise, rapt in her story, had not leaned forward to throw on fresh wood. The slender apple boughs in the grate were fragile arcs of ash. A fitful red light gleamed on the priest's shoes from one small heap of twigs that still burned.

Telling the story had calmed her down. The shivering and fever had gone. Tomorrow she would jump up and get on with her work. The illness which was the fear of hell had left her, and in its place she had a tale fitted together from chattering teeth, weeping, and sore bones, like a necklace that you string, in the order that most pleases you, with all the beads at your disposal. She held the ends in her hands, uncertain how to finish it. She had no idea how it would end. If Caroline returned to France one day, she might find out. She knew from Maître Robert, who had received a second letter from England, that Caroline had gone to America. She would have to wait, to see whether there would be any more news.

The priest went on snoring gently. He probably hadn't lis-

tened to a word she'd said. He was tired, and bored, not in the
mood to listen to the blatherings of a foolish woman.

It was the wrong story for him. Not his style. But his coming
to visit her had taught Louise one thing. Telling the story was
as important as what was in it. She needed an audience, and
tomorrow she would go out and find one and begin again.
Perhaps this time she would tell François, and the children.

Now you can order superb titles directly from Virago

☐	Flesh and Blood	Michèle Roberts	£6.99
☐	Impossible Saints	Michèle Roberts	£6.99
☐	All the Selves I Was	Michèle Roberts	£8.99
☐	During Mother's Absence	Michèle Roberts	£5.99
☐	Food, Sex & God	Michèle Roberts	£9.99
☐	Daughters of the House	Michèle Roberts	£6.99

Please allow for postage and packing: **Free UK delivery.**
Europe; add 25% of retail price; Rest of World; 45% of retail price.

To order any of the above or any other Virago titles, please call our credit card orderline or fill in this coupon and send/fax it to:

Virago, 250 Western Avenue, London, W3 6XZ, UK.
Fax 0181 324 5678   Telephone 0181 324 5516

☐ I enclose a UK bank cheque made payable to Virago for £ ....
☐ Please charge £.............. to my Access, Visa, Delta, Switch Card No.

☐☐☐☐☐☐☐☐☐☐☐☐☐☐☐☐☐☐☐

Expiry Date ☐☐☐☐   Switch Issue No. ☐☐

NAME (Block letters please) ....

ADDRESS ....

....

....

Postcode ....Telephone ....

Signature ....

Please allow 28 days for delivery within the UK. Offer subject to price and availability.

Please do not send any further mailings from companies carefully selected by Virago ☐